When Bill steals some of Dead Al's cremation cinders from the
SQUED (the Standard Quality Urnstyle Economic Dispose-all)
it's not long before he finds himself – courtesy of his Buick – in
Helhevland on the Other Side, where his heart is examined to
see if its cadavre substance passes the weighing test into the astral
world . . . Perplexed? Bill is. The plot thickens with the infamous
Monkey Trial (*evil*-lution v. fundamentalism), Richard Nixon's
heavenly defence of his earthly behaviour, more Bills, the Chorus
and, worst of all, hell-on-earth in the shape of a stool in Bill's
bar which Al endowed with never-ending free drinks . . .

SQUED is a brilliant black comedy about the punishment
of truth; it's dead funny, bizarre, idiosyncratic, unorthodox,
outlandish . . . There hasn't been a book like it since *Slaughter-
house Five*.

Praise for Richard Miller's *Snail*:

'*Snail*: is it enlightenment or madness or just plain fun?' Tom
Robbins

'At once delirious and serious. Cast in the form of a traditional
picaresque novel, a series of incredible adventures and misadven-
tures, it addresses the basic themes of immortality, death, reincar-
nation and the future of the species' William S. Burroughs

'This action-packed picaresque novel moves on the high ground
of the fantasy genre' *New York Times*

'A raunchy fantasy that nods towards Heller and Vonnegut and
then roars up and beyond . . . This freewheeling, mindboggling
emotion-shattering fable will make readers' flesh crawl, trigger
daytime nightmares, and, finally, leave them laughing' *Pub-
lishers Weekly*

SQUED

RICHARD MILLER

BLOOMSBURY

First published in Great Britain 1989

Bloomsbury Publishing Ltd, 2 Soho Square, London W1V 5DE

© Richard Miller 1989

A CIP catalogue record for this book is available from the British Library
ISBN 0 7475 0455 5

10 9 8 7 6 5 4 3 2 1

Phototypeset by Rowland Phototypesetting Ltd,
Bury St Edmunds, Suffolk
Printed and bound in Great Britain by
Richard Clay Ltd, Bungay, Suffolk

To our brothers and sisters in the
Soviet Union and our mutual dedication
to universal peace

PART ONE

DEAD   AL

*Some things are too serious to take seriously,
and too funny to laugh at.*

Alvin Allen Burke, Pacifica, California 1990

ONE

They burned Al last week and, today, we dumped his ashes into the sea.

Lucky Al is dead and gone.

His bar-stool remains.

His bar-stool *is* his remains.

He endowed it in his will.

Don't shit where you eat, he used to tell me. He doesn't eat here any more. Lucky Al is *dead*. That's okay. We're all following him down the same path. Wherever my old pal Al is, people are playful and happy. I'm having lively thoughts about death and the dead. Al used to advise me against drinking with people with broken noses. He was at once a hard-ass practical-man and a merry idealist. He thought endowing a bar-stool would be fun.

As for me, because I own this place, I won't have to sit on his stool. I get free drinks at all of them. Right now I'm sitting at the corner of the bar, next to the lucky stool, with a bowl of ice, a glass, and a quart of Jack Daniels, looking at a sign on the wall: Pool Rules. It doesn't rule me. At the moment booze does. Al was my mentor. I'm an old-timer too, but not as old as Dead Al was. Folks call me Bill. Me, I'm a bill collector. The endless struggle to collect my bar tabs yields half my living. If I could collect all my tabs and cash my bad checks, I'd be making more than a living, but who needs more? My bill collection will be my summa. At the moment this is my endowed stool. As for *the* endowed stool, everyone who sits on it can, in a manner of speaking, be me. As long as they sit there, they'll get free drinks, paid for by the endowment.

SQUED

Al's will stipulates the free-drink phase of his passage to the Other Side must begin the morning after his funeral, meaning a few hours from now.

What? Oh, yes, that's right, we're talking big money. Dead Al left a trust fund, *two hundred and seventy-eight grand* to be exact, to pay for drinks ordered by anyone sitting on the Dead Al Memorial Bar-stool. At the end of the fiscal year, May Fools' Day, the unspent income must be used to finance a Dead Al party. Starting at six a.m. we'll run a tab on that stool at our regular prices and each month the A.L. Foundation will pay it. What's that? You say you don't collect bills or Bills? You must save up something.

Stamps?

I think you'd like my place, though it would surely strike you as ordinary, round tables, beer signs, minimal bar food, a classic, flashing juke box. Comfort: that's the general atmosphere, sustained by honest drinks at honest prices, leavened with occasional excitement and just enough strangers to provide the fortuitous dimension. The bar-rail – a real railroad track – gives the place whatever claim it can make to distinction; that is, until stool fame spreads. Listening to radio music, seated – no perched here, gazing at the consecrated stool, I remembered Dead Al's will says free drinks may only be served to people named Bill. So most folks sitting there will become *honorary* Bills. That's all provided for in the will. The Will! How many Bills do I know? So here I sit, thumbing the index of my Bill collection, when, in fact, my real subject is death and the dead.

We never had a president named Bill. Okay. You're right. Bill Taft and Bill Harrison. Sure. And Bill McKinley, shot down in Buffalo. In fact, all those Bills are down with the deads. Bills. I own a painting by Bill Wiley. It's over there on the wall behind the pool table, by the list of rules. It depicts a school slate scrawled: I hope you learned your lesson. Chalk – real chalk – hangs from the painting on a string. And now I'm remembering Billy Bathgate, the story of an imaginary Al from the Bronx slums. This week I've been reading a novel following the career of Billy Phelan, an exalted loser, an unlucky Al.

Half a century of tobacco smoke and stale beer gives my saloon its aroma.

From here I can see the beach. I can see it from all the stools because when I remodeled and tore out the booths, I had them build a long window over the back bar where the beverage racks and mirror used to be. Before I opened up that grand panorama of sunset and beach, it was guilty dark in here. All you could see were dim reflections and bottles. Sometimes, while drinking after hours, the past and future collapsing into a foetal now, their labels hypnotized me. Whiskey/Whisky. BEEFEATER BEE FEATER. These days, instead of food for such schizoid thought, the back bar displays a stage where late at night, when lit by the moon, as at this moment, my mind's eye sees enchanted theater.

Right now – far upstage – the black, insect silhouette of a big ship creeps slowly along the horizon.

Dead Al used to hear Time's wingèd chariot hurtling near; he used to dream up ways to fête its arrival. In memory-vision I see him sitting on his stool, the one predestined for celebrity, gazing out at the sandy watery stage, picturing his own last rites, always moonlit. In a favorite fancy, cheered on by mourners, holding a cigar-box 'squed' containing Al's ashes, a sky-blue surfboard clenched under one arm, Al's great-grandson Billy Williams wades into the ocean. He lies on the board and pressing the squed down on it with his abdomen, paddles out beyond the break point where he waits, undulating, the squed in his hands. A big wave swells under him; he paddles up its back, stands, and riding the wave toward shore, raises the squed high, springs off the board, and vanishing in the spray, swims deep, empties the squed, pulls himself up and broaches the bubbling silvery surface, laughing and smiling, hair streaming.

Sea-otter style, he clutches the empty squed to his chest, and, moonlight gleaming on his belly, swims to the board, mounts it, and holding the squed aloft rides a curling wave crest back to the beach.

But that's not the way it turned out.

After all, you can't create the future.

    Al, though, always seemed to think you could: all it takes, said he, is decision, resolution, persistence, and plenty of TLC – you know, Tenacious Loyal Concern.

    With that in mind, Al endowed his wake and left the details and the TLC to me.

Sitting here one afternoon with an honorary Bill named Josh whose charter boat, a sixty-four foot sloop *Honorary Bill* – I mean *Ruby* but from now on I'll leave some of the Bills to your imagination – whose sloop *Ruby* rode at anchor just off the beach, while gazing at her and at the orange rubber dinghy Josh had rowed ashore, I suddenly saw the future. When Time's wingèd dinghy hurtled here and took Al aboard, we'd cremate what Al left behind, pack the ashes into a squed he himself had selected from the catalog, and, as the climax of a *fun*erary party aboard *Ruby*, Josh and I would scatter the ashes into the sea while the stereo blared the William Tell Overture as preface to the coming début of the diabolic stool and the dionysiac Dead Al Bacchanal Party: the twin phases of Al's everlasting wake.

    No statue smaller than Liberty could do as much to preserve his memory.

    There's nothing on the stage now. The sea, almost flat, lies silver under the moon. Today, my vision of the future came true, but not exactly as I'd foreseen. After the revels and solemnities, we disposed of Al's cremains. About sundown we returned to Frisco and after passing under the hooting, ringing, flashing drawbridge, we docked *Ruby* at the China Basin building and dispersed. I drove straight back here to Pacifica, alone, and let myself into my bar – closed for the day – to have a private drink with Al's memory. When we open at six a.m., I'll inaugurate his monumental stool. Al's ashes are now out beyond the stage, somewhere in the deep. I brought his squed back with me and set it on the sill of the view window, next to my binoculars, where it will catch sunshine. I'm going to plant something in it. Forget-me-nots? Don't need them, not with a perpetual wake in progress. A cactus, maybe? One whose sole moisture derives from whiskey? The squed, like *Ruby*, is made of steel. It's a six-inch cube enameled spinach-green, a sports-car finish densely rich in the glow of the bar-room nightlights.

Al's cremains looked like kitty litter.

He should have left them to his cat.

I promised Al that when he died I'd take his body to the Neptune Society to be burned, then arrange for the goodbye funeral aboard *Ruby*. The timing could be loose, spontaneous. Ashes, after all, are easier to keep than corpses. You don't need a freezer to preserve gravel. Another reason Al was so keen on cremation is he could not stand the idea of being half buried and half thrown out with the garbage. Embalmed, he said, his remains would be a shell, devoid of blood, guts, brains, heart. They'd save his appearance, but trash his character. They'd scoop him out like a Christmas goose and give what remained of his remains the taxidermy treatment. They would not even leave a bag of token giblets inside. Would they mount him for display? No. They'd pack Stuffed Al into a box to molder. They'd hide Boxed Al in a hole, never more to be seen until some twenty-first-century developer, raising the dead, dug Al up while excavating a telephone trench.

The very thought of caskets and coffins gave him the creeps.

Yes, of course, they give you the creeps too.

But, beyond all that, Al had a special reason.

Years ago, when he was treasurer of the Community Democratic Club, we often helped the party raise money. The mortician who used to own the parlors across the road seemed a prime prospect because he wanted to become postmaster when the incumbent postmaster retired. He could thus exit gracefully from the death biz. In our view his chief rival was another wealthy, middle-aged man, a gynecologist we call Doc, who also looked on the post office as a dignified refuge from a loathsome profession.

Since then, the mummy-maker has passed to the Other Side. Perhaps he's fulfilled his ambition in Hell. Yes, he's postmaster general. What do Hell stamps look like? What do the locals paste on their letters, and what's the postage to the States? The UK? The regular issue includes the ultramarine 6-cent Beelzebub, the vermilion 12-cent Belial, the magenta 18-cent Lucifer, the turquoise 66-cent Samiel, the carmine $6.66 Mephistopheles, the sepia $66.60 Set, and the sable $666.00 Satan. And what about commemoratives? Sold in six-by-six sheets bound in six-sheet books, we have the Fall from Heaven issue, and, in coils of six hundred and sixty-six, the Beast Mark issue. But no, wait ... that's not an *issue*, it's a medium of exchange. Beast Marks, BM's, not dollars or francs or pounds, are the money in Hell. There's the Devil's Surrogates issue, denominated in BM's, showing all the Popes and Metropolitans; the 666 Demons of Distinction, the Prince of Darkness, Fiery Fiends, Succubi, Vampires –

What?

> *Old Al's dead and gone,*
> *Left us here to sing his song;*
> *Old Al's dead and gone,*
> *Left us here to sing his song.*

Those warblers over there? Yes, I see them too, near the wall, in the shadows, sitting on the pool table.

Who are they?

'They're the Enkidu and Winnetou Club Chorus.'

The choristers wait for applause, which I supply, and then they burst into another song.

> *They're moving Alvin's grave to build a sewer;*
> *They're moving it regardless of ex-pense;*
> *They are shifting his re-mains,*
> *To make room for ten-inch drains,*
> *To bleed off some toff's fine res-i-dence!*

'You didn't want that future, did you Al?'

My mind's eye sees obscure forms fixed in a phantom mirror and bottles racked in murky ranks.

It's too dark in this place.

Some day I'll make a view window back there; I'll remodel.

But I'll keep these stools. They're the old kind, the kind that spin. Basically, they're discs upholstered with maroon leather, skirted with art-deco chromed steel, and supported by pylons firmly rooted in the floor. They've been here since 1940 – much longer than I have. No wonder they look so ragged.

BEEFEATER. BEE FEATER.

Whiskey/Whisky.

Al and Doc are standing next to me. Perched on the stool beside me is W. B. Antonelli, the funeral director. They're gulping free drinks my barmaid keeps serving. As for me, I'm sipping, so if Al and I can persuade them to contribute to the Democrats, I'll be in condition to rush to the bank and slide their checks into the night-deposit slot and thwart the possible effects of morning-after thought. Al's getting sloppy. He just referred to W.B. as an undertaker.

'How many times do I have to tell you I'm a *mortician*?'

'Beautician?' says Al, reverting to his Missouri accent. 'I'll bet you're a real whiz at permanent waves.'

He doffed his hat, a Mexican hat, and set it on the bar. Today he was a Mexican rancher. He'd come in homeward bound from a costume party and run into W.B. and Doc. He was pretty drunk, but unless he walked, most people couldn't tell. 'Imagine, boys, I'm still incognito, still wearing my Venetian domino.' He ordered a zombie astral, one made with vodka, because he preferred it to the zombie cadavre, made with rum. He waved hello to a woman coming in the door. 'Let's hear it for Two Twelve Heather,' he said in his normal voice, which was at once cultivated and common.

'Two *Ton* Heather,' said W.B.

'Respect the ladies, dead and alive.'

Two Twelve Heather approached, carrying something in a seabag I recognized as Al's. A member of the National Maritime Union since helping to organize it in the thirty-six strike, Al had sailed as able-bodied seaman and bosun from the middle twenties until the early sixties, which is to say he'd earned a PhD at Down Home U. He'd read thousands of the books placed aboard ships by the Seamen's Church Institute. He'd ranged the ports of the world and participated in countless messroom colloquies with shipmates from most of its nations. 'Catch that, she's smiling like a mule eating briars.' Me, I've been around the block a few times, too, but nothing like Al. Yet *I'm* the one with a tattoo: on the back of my watch hand, a small, blue anchor. Al flashes a gold tooth. Heather claims no matter what she does or doesn't do, like fast, like pray, like exercise, she always weighs two hundred and twelve pounds.

'Bandito mio!' she said to Al.

'Try ranchero.'

'How 'bout a kiss?'

'I'd smother you.'

'No way. Two of you wouldn't make one of me.' She'd come to return Al's medieval-style mandolin. Al called it a lute. He'd made it himself, years before, and he loved to play it with tumultuous abandon while crooning shit-kicking incendiary songs through his tight, nasty smile. At rest, he looked a bit soft, but once in motion the energy flaring through him created a demon, an incubus. She pushed up against him. 'Kiss me and I'll send you a love letter.'

'Better than that, send me a mammogram.' He reached into her cleavage and tweaked a nipple. She presented him the lute.

'Play us a song.'

'Can't think of one.'

'What's your favorite?'

'Drop-Kick Me, Jesus, Through the Goal Posts of Life.' Al passed the lute to me. 'Take it before I fall on it and make some smithereens.' I hung it on the wall at the end of the bar, its usual place, next to his musical saw. I see them both there now, an Alivarius and a Sandvik, waiting to sing for new masters.

Two Twelve Heather called for zombies astral all 'round. 'I'm celebrating, folks. Got my new vanity plates today.'

'Teeth?'

'No, not teeth, sweetie. License plates for my car. 212 LBS. How's that for an easy number to remember?' She turned to W.B. 'When old father Fat Sucker catches up with me and cuts me down, I mean when I croak, I want to be planted in my car. Glue my plates to my gravestone. Bury me in my car.'

'What?'

'Don't look at me like that. I got the mon. I'll pay you in advance so you don't have to use no celestial collection agency.'

'Well, I don't know . . . '

'The moment I saw you here, I decided I want you to handle the arrangements. Make it fancy, Mr. Antonelli, de-luxe. And don't forget to fasten the seat belt. On my way to heaven, I don't want to roll around, or get busted by sky police, or have Saint Peter call me a scofflaw, nope, not me.' Two Twelve Heather ordered more zombies astral, two for Al, who'd stumbled off to piss, and two to fuel her impetuous driving habits which, as she explained, she hoped would eventually produce a crash of sufficient violence to cost her a limb and thus substantially reduce her weight. 'As I always say, when you're sweating off that avoirdupois, the last fifty pounds are the hardest.'

The zombies came and she turned her back on W.B. and Doc. They conferred quietly about something that made them laugh out loud. Al lurched across the floor from the can and leaned against William Broderick Antonelli III, fearless funeral director.

'It's about time you put some life in your death biz,' Al said.

To break down their reluctance to financing the Democracy, he'd been matching them drink for drink.

'Go into cremation! Get in on the ground floor! It's the wave of the future, of the twenty-first century! Buy your own retort and cook them down yourself. Get out ahead of the fire craze and you can sell pre-need burn plans to everyone in town! You'll get richer than a ton of steer manure and, out of gratitude to me, you can give a tithe of your loot to the Democrats. We'll all help, won't we?' This last to me.

'Sure. I always do what I can for a good, deserving Democrat.'

'Those Neptunes,' said W.B., 'get much less than a grand for the whole job. Me, I can make more than twice that much on the casket alone.'

'Cremation! Foresight! Jump in while there's money to be made. Think thermonuclear. Cremation's the coming thing. Take your profits before some generous government gives us all a pre-need burn, free! Right now, most Brits leave the world via Chimney Street. Swedes, too. They're practical, aesthetic. They're like me. You can throw me down Vesuvius or into the Boiling Mud Pools of Rotorua, but you'll never get me into one of your boxes, never.'

'Cremation's a fad,' said Doc. 'Nothing more.'

'Ah, me, so it is: the trendy burn, garbage disposal à la mode.' Al winked at W.B. 'No need to comb the hair on their arms to make them look pretty.'

'You don't see their arms.'

'In that case, cut them off and feed them to your dogs.' He turned back to Doc. 'I see a conflict of interest here. Why can't you see it? You should burn your mistakes, but this here honey-fugler wants to mummify them, preserve them forever, and make big bucks doing it.'

'Al,' said W.B., 'I'm getting sick and tired of your fault finding.'

'Fault finding? I'd say it's more like shit storming.'

'I work hard, all the time. You think it's easy? Well, it's not! And it's depressing, too. I deserve every penny I get.'

'That's right,' said Doc.

'Okay. I'm convinced. Our pal here makes his money the old-fashioned way. He urns it.'

W.B. glanced at Doc. 'He's asking for it.' Doc nodded: Oh yes he is. Doc and W.B. put Al's arms around their shoulders and walked him toward the door. Two Twelve Heather tugged his sombrero tightly down on to his head.

'Alvin Burke! On your stumbling staggering homeward lurch you better not sashay through no hog pens, 'cause you'll slip on shit and they'll eat you.'

'And solve my death problem free, and make my monument a ham sandwich.' He straightened, then sagged back on to his prosthetic pals. 'No hogs here, babe. Just Billy-boy's parlors.'

'Yes,' said W.B. He spoke to me. 'You're going to walk him around for a while before we take him home.' At the door, he paused and called back. 'We're going to teach this wise guy a lesson.'

TWO

I'm still roosting here waiting for six a.m. and the stool's début. Roosting? More like rooted here. I'm a stool potato. That's it, a stool potato. Solid, but overweight. So, what the hell? Who ever heard of a potato with hair, even thin sandy hair going gray. Right now I'm looking at Al's obituary. I spilled some whiskey on it. It's a clipping from the San Mateo *Times*, about two weeks old, 28 April 1990. It's not precisely an obituary, though. It's actually a news story. Papers like the *Times* don't print obits of ordinary folks.

DEATH TAKES 'LUCKY' AL

The oldest man ever to win a major prize in a state lottery died last night in his sleep at the age of eighty-three. Born in 1907 in Boonville, Mo., Alvin Allen Burke was known to his friends as 'Lucky Al' even before August of 1987 when at the age of eighty he won $355,000.

Burke, a retired merchant seaman, is best remembered for his long, successful struggle to obtain a court order directing the state to pay him all the money at once instead of in increments over an extended period.

According to William Williams, a great-grandson who lived with him: 'Alvin Burke believed himself the last American whose favorite president is Warren G. Harding. Harding appealed to him because of all the presidents – Reagan included – he was the one who really knew how to bloviate.'

That's all. That's it. A proper obituary of Al, one listing the jobs he's had and the things he's done and the places he's been and the ladies he's loved would fill a whole page of the *Times*. Imagine! This clipping will yellow and crumble. But, barring the mass-crumble of World War III, the *Times* itself marches on and will outlive us all.

Now I'm gazing at Al's squed and the black sky beyond. Out there on *Ruby* I cheated. Not all of Al's ashes are in the sea. I kept some, and mixed them with dirt from the garden out in front of my club where the baby palm tree is, and packed this Al soil into his squed. His visible monument will be a plant, not a slab, or a ham sandwich. So I'm gazing at his squed waiting for the advent of a green shoot. Maybe it will speak to me. Maybe his ashes will. His ashes? No. All that's left after cremation is five to seven pounds of bone chips.

W.B. told me the kitty litter is pure bone.

About an hour after W.B. and Doc led Al out, they came back chuckling and smirking. Al had opened the money can all right. Here was a heaven-sent opportunity and a patriotic duty to do some honey-fugling of my own and suck out a solid contribution.

They ordered zombies cadavre.

I declined a refill.

'Where's Al?'

'He's at home, his once and future home,' Doc replied.

'We decided at his age it's time to ease him into it.'

'Boys,' said I, 'he *is* eased into it. He's lived over there on Pine for twenty years.'

They both flashed shit-eating grins and kept on drinking.

They seemed to be waiting for something.

I loosed a torrent of money-raising blather on them, assailed them with innuendo suggesting this was the first phase of the postmastership auction. They each gave me checks for five hundred bucks, mainly to shut me up.

W.B. raised his glass to Doc.

'Get 'em while they're hot!'

Doc clicked glasses.

'Get 'em while they're hot!' said W.B. to me.

'Who?'

'Them.'

'Them?'

'Clients. Get them while they're hot. That's our motto, our professional motto. Not warm. No sir. Hot!' He exploded into gleeful laughter. 'That one, Doc . . . yes . . . we'll never get one any hotter than *that*.'

'No indeed.'

'Supple. You want them supple. Subtle, eh?' W.B. put his hand on Doc's shoulder. 'Like this one client we had. Died five miles above the Rockies in an airplane seat. No one noticed until all the other passengers had walked off. Rigor mortis had set in. Believe me, R M can be one big pain in the ass.'

'So can spending half your life looking up vaginas,' said Doc.

'We had a suicide yesterday. Hung himself. I don't know what this generation's coming to. No pride. People used to have a sense of craftmanship. Style. Even when they killed themselves it showed. This young kid, he didn't take suicide – or himself for that matter – seriously. He didn't even use a neck-breaking knot. No. He stood on a chair in his garage, tied an extension cord around his neck and to a beam, kicked the chair out, and swung there choking. No research, no planning, no rehearsals. I put the finishing touches on him this afternoon.'

'Is that the corpse on the table next to Al?'

'The one and the same.'

'I remember thinking Al must have looked like that fifty years ago.'

'Lighter hair, probably. And Al's a little taller. He must be nearly six feet.'

SHAME SHAME SHAME, chanted the Enkidu & Winnetou Club Chorus.

Al came in the door, pale, sober, looking like he'd just been shot.

He approached with an air of cold ferocity.

And him almost seventy.

'Bring Al a double,' W.B. cried out to the barmaid. 'He looks like he needs it.'

Al stood before them, silent, furious. He fixed W.B. with a raging glare.

'I'll bury you.'

He stalked out before I could show him our plunder.

They fall all over themselves trying to get me to absolve them for what they've done. The E & W Chorus squats there on the pool table chanting SHAME SHAME at the memory. Al's pals, it seems, walked Al directly across the road to W.B.'s Restful Garden Mortuary Chapel. I've known them both for years. I could just see them in action. W.B. turned on the musak. He fetched a bottle of whiskey and led them to a desk in the sales salon where, among the caskets and squeds and ceramic urns and shrouds and frontal suits and dresses for clothing the dead and brochures for Pre-Need Funeral Plans and enterprises like Air Hearse, Inc., they socialized and drank whiskey until Al passed out.

'So we put Al in my best casket, a half-couch model with satin cushions, and wheeled him into the slumber room where I have that kid laid out. We left the musak on and the lights, too, real dim, and came back here.'

As Al put it weeks later, sitting on his favorite stool, the stool God had destined for endowment, 'If you got a blood transfusion from that pill roller, or, for that matter, from our favorite bier baron, you'd turn into a rat.' He says all his salty, down-home stuff in his usual cultivated way, but touched with his Missouri accent and a flash of gold tooth. 'Those two guys, when they come to see you they don't knock, they just slide in under the door.'

And then, suddenly, he was talking about his own death.

That was quite unlike him.

'Bill, in some ways I feel closer to you than I do to anyone else. Those two intestine-colored gang-greened sons-of-bitches laying me out in a coffin like that! I tell you, I am absolutely resolved that when death grabs my ass I'm going to be *burned*, not buried. I'll ride the flames to the spirit world, not lie there like a piece of beef jerky waiting for the fucking worms.'

His voice, abruptly, became soft and tired.

'When I sat up in that coffin and saw where I was . . . Oh, man! Promise me, when my time comes, and at my age that could be any day now, promise me you'll make sure I'm cremated, and then you'll make them dump the cinders into the sea.'

'Count on me.'

'You'll burn me down to bone meal, you promise?'

'Absolutely.'

We shook on it.

He told me – and this was before he won the lottery – his net worth, not counting his house, was thirty grand. He would leave his house and twenty grand to his only surviving descendant, Bill Williams. 'That boy loves the sea as much as I do, and he rides it on a surfboard, which is getting one hell of a lot closer to it than you do on ships. That kid's like me. He has *style*. Surfing's beautiful. I've never done it, but it sure is something to watch. Beautiful. Not competitive. Philosophical. Just you on the flexing muscle of the sea. It's an artist's sport, just you and nature.'

I think of my saloon as a friendly neighborhood club and that's the way I run it. Bill Williams comes in here sometimes. I know he's only twenty, but, when it's safe, because he's so serene, I serve him anyhow. I remember once some aging hero, a superannuated adolescent, after insulting Billy and surfers until I was about ready to toss him out, told Billy, 'You know what the trouble with you punk kids, with America, is? No balls. No fucking balls!'

Billy gave him a sunny smile. 'On the contrary, America has more balls than anybody.'

'Bull*shit*.'

'Just think of them all, you quintessential megageek! Balls! Billions of balls! Base and foot and tennis and basket and bowling and volley and rugby and soccer. Golf and pool and hand and ping and pong and bill and yard and you name it.'

I agree with Al. Billy's got it all right. So I told Al what a great kid Billy is, and I'm glad he's leaving his house and his money to Billy, but what of the other ten grand? 'Who gets that?'

'I don't know who gets it, but I do know what I'm going to *do* with it. I'm going to make me a monument that will keep me around, that will keep reminding Billy and my pals I'm still here, in spirit. I read about a new freeze-dry process that makes flawless mummies. Imagine! A man could be like the ancient Romans and their busts of ancestors, only better. He could have all his forebears sitting around the living room. If the process is available, spend the ten grand freeze-drying me. You can set me on this stool, permanently, for everyone to admire.'

'We could even wire you for sound.'

'But if the process's not ready in time, I want the ten grand offered as a cash prize for the first person who can break all ten commandments without breaking the law.'

How's that for a game?

The idea still echoes in my head.

Wouldn't that be something!

Rain carried by swirling wind is lunging out of the blackness against my view window. It hardly ever rains at all in May, let alone like that. A few hours ago, out there on the bay and the ocean, squalls kept hitting us, trying to keep us from dumping Al. Before Billy dove deep with the squed to release Al's bone chips, just before that, on impulse, I scooped out a pound or so, which is up there by the window in the squed, safe from the torrents buffeting the glass.

As I said before, I brought some Al home.

The part that survived fire and water.

And now, abruptly, eerily, it's clear out there; a moonlit vista has opened across the beach and sea to the horizon.

And I'm perched here listening to the Chorus sing 'Amazing Grace' and thinking about balls, great mounds of them, massy lumps of rubber bands, and skins puffed full of wind, and skulls, too, ranged in immense Persian drifts and enormous Celtic ridges all the way across America to the Atlantic.

SQUED

About thirty years ago, on a hot day like this, while walking uphill from here to the Enkidu & Winnetu Club, I spied a pool ball rolling toward me in the gutter. I caught it up, saving it from the sewer. I can feel its weight in my hand. I remember it as orange. Would that be the five? I should glance over at my table, but I'd rather imagine it. That's how I met Dead Al. He was standing in the doorway of the E & W, watching me field his ball. He'd blasted it right out into the street. When I handed it back to him he smiled that thin ragged-toothed smile and thanked me. He looked just like he did two weeks ago, only thirty years younger.

He sure looks different now.

Tossing the ball from hand to hand he said, 'By house rules that makes me a loser. Come on in; I'll buy you a beer.' He set the ball on its table, paid his bet, and told me he always hits the balls hard. He thinks slopping them in by soft touches is demeaning. He calls his style of game Viking pool. He usually wins, too. That's where he got the name Lucky Al. A white cotton cap like those you used to see on the waterfront slanted across his forehead. He called it his West Coast Stetson. That was May of 1960. The news columns and airwaves were fat with reports about police in San Francisco firehosing students down the marble staircase in the rotunda of City Hall where they'd come to harass hearings being conducted by the House Unamerican Activities Committee. A photo of this bizarre scene occupied the entire front page of the *Chronicle*. You might remember, that event marked the end of the sleepy fifties and was the overture of the crazy sixties. As quaint and surreal as it may seem, the House of Representatives really *did* have an Unamerican Activities Committee. And the feds refused to admit the existence of China. People then seemed generally to think that whenever you said *no* to authority your handle was being pulled in Moscow. Even in those days I suspected that that duck took wing not from the pinnacles of truth, but from the pleasure domes of the authorities. Because it was dangerous to express such thoughts in bars, I kept them to myself. Nowadays, in bars, you can say anything you damn please. Al, however, that thin smile stretched across his face, always said what he pleased, everywhere.

Al raised his beer glass to me and old Enkidu, and in a loud, musical voice, said, 'Here's to them kick-ass kids in Frisco.'

I clicked glasses with him.

'For sure.'

Old Enkidu gave him an angry look.

'And to the Dani tribe in New Guinea.'

'New Guinea?' said our kindly host.

'Just paid off a ship that stopped at Port Moresby.'

'Where's that?'

'New Guinea.'

'New Guinea?'

'Yes. We went out to Australia, up to New Guinea, then stopped in New Zealand on our way back to Frisco, where those kids are kicking ass. I walked on their picket line yesterday. Five thousand people were pe-ram-bu-lating a-round City Hall. One of them was Albert Einstein's grand-daughter.'

'Fucking treason, if you ask me.'

'Didn't ask you.'

Right then I decided this guy – this Al – is something *else*.

'You're getting on thin ice,' said old Enkidu.

Al smiled at me, turned back to our kindly host.

'In the beginning was the Hole.'

'What?'

'It all began with the Hole. First, out of the Hole came the Dani men. Around the mouth of the Hole they found rich soil, and they cultivated that soil. Then pigs came out of the Hole. The Dani men mastered the pigs and treasure them to this day. Then women came out of the Hole. The Dani men mastered them, too.'

'Jesus.'

'Not yet. Then more men came out of the Hole. Portuguese led by Jesus. Spaniards, Dutch, Brits, Aussies, Japs, Americans, then commies. No room was left around the Hole, so the newcomers ranged out over the world, questing for land as good as the Dani land, for a Hole as good as the Dani Hole. But they didn't find either one.'

Al ordered more beer.

Old Enkidu poured it, having mellowed considerably.

'And you know what? They all started coming back. And you know what happened then?'

'No, what happened?'

'They moved the Hole to Frisco and more commies came out, striking fear into the hearts of the timid. Ever since then, we've had commiphobes like you.'

Ever since that, Al and I have been friends, and regulars at the Enkidu & Winnetou.

We were last there in April.

When Al passed through to the Other Side – his ticket was a heart attack, and I'll bet right now he's tuned-in to all of this – I phoned the Neptune Society and said we'd bring them his body. About noon that day Bill Williams had rushed into my place, and called me over, and told me Al hadn't come down for breakfast, or to read the paper, and that he'd finally gone upstairs, and found Al spread out face down on the floor of his room, dead, 'just like in some copy show on TV.' As we ran around the corner and under the shade trees on Pine, I envisioned Al's oaken floor, and saw chalked on it an outlined Al resembling what people draw on walks and buildings for Hiroshima Day. We dashed into the house and up the stairs and there lay Al clad in orange briefs, pale, supple, dead. Three days later the Neptunes called me and told me to come pick up his ashes. I drove out there and got the squed-full of Al chips. Most of him, by then, had risen high in the air, diffusing into the jet stream. How many years will Al be falling out of the sky on to lands and seas? Will Al's molecules circulate forever in the ozone layer, or even flip out into space? I locked his squed into my trunk along with some coke cans and oil bottles and the spare tire and a bag of tools, and drove home, breathing an atmosphere recently enriched by free Al-ecules. Then Billy and I got together with Josh and set a date for Al's burial at sea. I went about my business for a week or so, and forgot about Al riding back there in the trunk. Yesterday I dropped in at the E & W. Bill (honorary) Enkidu II brought me the usual.

'Where's Al? I owe him a drink.'

'How come?'

'The Cards beat the Giants.'

He and Al had a standing bet on Cardinal-Giants games. He gave me some nuts. 'So where the hell is he?'

'Just a minute. I'll go get him.'

I went to my car, opened the trunk, and took out the squed. I went back in and placed it on the bar.

'What's that?'

'A squed.'

'What's a squed?'

'SQUED's an acronym body burners use for what is more formally known in their trade as Standard Quality Urnstyle Economical Dispose-all. Cardboard squeds they call UU's for Utility Urns, you know, you you.'

'So where's Al?'

'Right here.'

'Nobody here but you and that squed.'

'Just set up Al's drink.'

'Okay, if you say so.'

Enkidu II poured a double shot and set it on the bar.

'Well, where is he?'

'You're looking at him.'

I opened the squed, exposing the Al-ecules still yet earth-bound, and poured in the booze.

I'll do it. I'll plant something in it that thrives on bourbon.

I'm hovering here, feeling no pain, Bill-ecules spreading out from me into my big box of a family saloon.

I'm in my box just like Al's in his.

Only he ain't.

I'm listening to the Chorus sing about me to the tune of 'Paddy Murphy'.

> *The night that Al Burke died,*
> *We never will forget,*

Old Bill he got stinkin' drunk,
And he sure ain't sober yet!

And now they're sliding back to Paddy's fatal eve:

They did a thing that awful night,
That filled my heart with fearrrrrr,
They took the ice right off the corpse
And put it on the beer. Hey!

Flickering on the movie screen on the back of my forehead I
see another chorus. Afrika Korps prisoners swing along to an
exuberant liquid marching song. We're in Camp Ellis, Illinois,
where I spent most of the war, an adolescent soldier in the
army engineers. See me up there on the screen, marching with
my chorus, Charley Company.

Count cadence, count!
One, two, three, four, one two
THREE FOUR!

Sound off!
Jody's cunt is rotten bait,
Just what we appreciate!
Sound off!
THREE FOUR!

So, anyway, back there at the E & W, in 1960, fielding a pool
ball, that's how I first said hello to Al. As for goodbye, this
afternoon Bill Williams and I went over to San Francisco, to
the Bay where *Ruby* is berthed. Al had survived all of his
intimates but us two. Consequently, us two are all who
rode out on *Ruby*, except for her captain, Josh, a sturdy
rusty-haired guy, a water-lover just like Billy. We'd timed it
so Al's last trip would fade into the sunset. Billy's got to be
the premier water baby. He was body surfing before he could
walk. He dotes on water polo and competition swimming.
He loves to don a wetsuit and aqualung and sound down

into that other world beneath the waves. He waterskis and windsurfs. As for *Ruby*, whom he greatly admires, she's long and thin. A single mast carries her sails. Billy and I helped set the mainsail and jib. I'm clumsy at it. Al and Billy were born to it. And here I was, taking Al's place. We went out through the Golden Gate, then steered for the sun, by now a flaming five-ball orange, and watched it roll down between tall clouds. You could see rain slanting gray from them to the water.

Billy and I sat barefoot in warm air, backs to the wheel-house, Al between us, deep in thought. Sharing an impulse, we stripped off our raingear. The deck inclined beneath us, pitching a little. A squall rushed over us, a wet force, blinding, drenching, bracing. The line between air and water had abruptly diffused and we two amphibians, streaming with water, clad only in shorts, transported to another world, exalted.

And suddenly, as sudden as our entry, we were back out on the water under blue sky watching the five-ball slide toward the horizon.

We dropped the sails and drifted on long swells.

'You know what?' Josh asked as we joined him by the wheel, 'last winter, I think it was at the E & W, some gal asked Al to what does he attribute his old age. He tells her, "I carry a loaded pistol, drink a quart of rum a day, and, so's not to miss anything, nights I never sleep more than two hours."'

I scooped a handful of Al out of the squed and put it into a styrofoam cup and stashed it to pick up later.

Billy and I walked out to the bow.

We sat down on the deck by the prow, feet swinging over the side catching spray, our arms resting on the chain rail, Al between us. Billy put Al on his lap.

'Al told me a kid like me feels immortal, but getting old you begin to feel temporary, a visitor, a tourist. The world becomes a motel with an indefinite check-out time.'

We watched the sun decline.

'Al told me sailors feel themselves strangers in every

country, especially their own. They only feel at home in the worldwide nation of ships and the sea.'

The wind subsided to a breath.

The sea's surface, just below our feet, lay smooth, viscous, transparent, and, beneath it, nothing moved.

'Al told me life is a game. You make your moves, play your cards, invent them when you can. The win? We win when all of us – everyone, everywhere, is living in peace and freedom, in harmony with all life.'

Al time had come.

I took Al's squed from his great-grandson, and as it weighed in my hands and I gazed down into the water, I sensed another surface and a different deep, and down in it somewhere a bubble, a vacuum where Al used to be.

'Al did everything I just dreamed of doing.'

Billy smiles at me.

'You ain't dead yet.'

The sun sinks.

Billy stands, mounts the rail, springs from the rail into the sea.

He broaches and reaches up to me. I hand him the squed.

Treading, he holds the squed aloft, his legs foreshortened by water.

'Goodbye, Al,' I call out. 'Goodbye.'

Billy flipped and plunged.

He vanished into the murk, and as I sat there alone, looking at the ripples he left behind, at liquid void, I imagined a blood cloud and the thrashing violence of a great white shark.

THREE

I'm still saying goodbye. I'm really filling this place. The walls are my skin. I'm thinking of a rope now. One strand twisted into the rest of my life, like the red strand in Royal Navy rope, will be the goodbye-to-Al strand. Yes. It begins back in 1960, that Al strand, and reaches out ahead. A fortnight ago it broke. No, it wasn't that. Nor did it end and re-begin. No. It changed color. Orange to . . . what?

Nostalgia is a memory wallow. That's what Al called it. But nostalgia's what I feel.

'When I was a boy,' he said, probably to hold my nose to the spinning reality-stone, 'people found fingers and mice in their canned meat.'

Wallow in that!

So, okay, I hear you. You're pretending they buried Al so you can finish your song about moving his grave to build a sewer.

> *Alvin in his life was n'er a quitter,*
> *And we don't believe he'll be a quitter now;*
> *Oh, he'll rise up in his sheets,*
> *And haunt those shithouse seats,*
> *And only let them shit when he'll al-low!*

How many graves worldwide have been shifted in the interests of sewage? They moved all the cemeteries out of San Francisco years ago.

> *Won't there be some bloody con-sti-pa-tion?*
> *Won't those bastards r-ant and rave?*

> *But it's only what they deserve*
> *To have the bloody nerve*
> *To bugger up a union workman's grave!*

Even though he lived partly on investments, Al always thought of himself as a working stiff.

'They boiled King Henry V down to bones,' said Al, 'and a regal procession conducted the bones from Paris to London to bury them in Westminster Abbey.' People used to tell Al he should write a book, and he'd say he was. 'My book is called J-H-V-H. It's the biography of a cruel and merciless two-bit desert war god who fought his way to the top. You know: The working class can kiss my ass, I've got the foreman's job at last!'

I can see King Henry's procession filing along the beach outside my view window, walking on the hard, wet sand where the waves wash, the latest in the Pageant Series on my de-luxe, wide-screen TV. My business sense tells me to build a transparent barrel vault over the terrace on the other side of the window and make myself a world-class view lounge and restaurant, but I won't, because it would ruin my view from here.

'A toast to Clarence Darrow,' Al says, interrupting my thoughts. 'A pledge.'

I lift my glass to Clarence Darrow.

A composite of Eugene Debs, Andrew Furuseth, Mark Twain, and Clarence Darrow had served adolescent Al as his model of manhood. A sceptic, an agnostic surely, an atheist perhaps, Darrow had promised a close friend if, indeed, an after-world exists, on the anniversary of his death he, Darrow, would return from it to report. Death came; a year passed. The friend vigiled from midnight to midnight, and in the right time-zone too, but detected nothing extraordinary.

After telling me this story, Al had said when he died, as soon as he was accustomed to the Other Side, he'd come back to visit me. He would not pass through a radar dish or cathode-ray tube, come as a radio voice or a TV image. No. He would appear in person.

'When it's time to inaugurate my catastrophe stool, I'll be back.'

'Okay.'

'About dawn.'

'Whatever you say, Al. You know I don't believe in necromancy.'

In June of 1925 the students in his high school elected Al as their president to serve during the 1925-1926 academic year. 'When I think back on those days,' he says, 'I see tire swings, coopers' hoops, taped baseballs, Halloween pranks, ice skates, spud games, scabbed knees, cops-and-robbers, firecrackers, snowball fights, king-of-the-mountain, drooping knee socks, Flexible-Flyer sleds, rubber-band airplanes, barrel-stave hammocks, balloon-tired bikes, woolen bathing suits, cotton dresses, pet snakes, strip poker, pea-shooters, skinny-dipping, tree-climbing, river-rafting, rabbit hunting; cap pistols, ragged sneakers, soapbox racers, Louisville sluggers, baseball cards, giant catfish, hidden clubhouses. And now, year after year, life gets more organized. Children don't invent their own amusements any more, nor do they live in their own separate world. No! Today it's Little League and T V. Today it's parents prying into every secret, adults hypnotizing the young, keeping them under constant surveillance – crushing their spirits, grinding their nuts! Order. That's where it's going. Not law, *order*. Anthill order. A big yes-sir no-sir hive of self-programming robots!'

'I've noticed it too.'

'And yet despite all that, the world has never built a better lad than Bill Williams.'

'Yes, Al. Bill Williams. I move we elect him to represent us in the life of the twenty-first century.'

The big story in the spring of 1925 was the Scopes trial to be held that summer in Dayton, Tennessee. William Jennings Bryan was to help prosecute John T. Scopes for telling high-school students about what Bryan referred to as *evil*-ution. Scopes had thus broken the new law against teaching anything but the Biblical story of creation. Among the squadrons of newsmen covering would be H. L. Mencken himself. Al had not given the question of evolution much thought one way or another. God and the Bible generated feelings of awe in him; Hell produced its terrors. In bed waiting for sleep, he prayed for his parents and for his sister who'd drowned in the river; he prayed for delivery from the boredom of life in Boonville and from the duty of submitting to Sunday morning church services. Afternoons and Saturdays, and now that school was out, six days a week, he worked at the landing loading and unloading steamboats, all the while suffering an intense envy of all those on board as the boats thrashed away to go up the Missouri to Kansas City and beyond, or run down to the Mississippi . . . and down that vast brown river to Saint Louis where his grandfather lived, and to Memphis and Natchez and Baton Rouge and . . . New Orleans!

'All my life my mother had struggled to make me a loyal member of the Methodist Episcopal Church. When, finally, I asked her what the Method is, the Method that distinguishes it from the Baptists and Presbyterians and Lutherans and the rest, she could not tell me. She didn't know! She didn't know what she believed, what she nagged me to believe. Ignorance and hypocrisy *that* profound is enough to . . . to make the angels weep. I'd saved some money. The newspaper stories about Darrow and Bryan and evolution and creation had given me a focus, a destination. And my excuse? As president of the student body it was up to me to go to Dayton, Tennessee, learn the truth, then come back and tell it to the whole school, teachers and all.

'Monkey Trial, *here I come*!'

FOUR

He tugged on his baseball cap – crimson for the Cardinals; he slung a blanket roll over his shoulder and slamming the screen door behind him, stalked out of the house. I can see Al dressed in corduroy knickerbockers, knee socks, and smelly ankle-high canvas sneakers, Keds, as he strides across the porch, down the steps, and along the walk out to the street.

A shouting argument with his father as to whether he was old enough to wear long pants had provided the impetus.

When he got to Memphis he would buy a pair.

Whistling, tossing a baseball, he walked along the dusty street toward the bluff and the road leading down to the landing.

The ball had entered Al's life in 1915 in Saint Louis as a foul from the bat of Rogers Hornsby. It dropped into the bleachers where his grandfather had taken him to see the Cardinals play the Cubs.

His grandfather had caught the ball and given it to him. Just last Christmas, Al gave his lucky ball to Bill Williams.

Ramble, oh didn't he ramble,
In and out of town,
Ramble, oh didn't he ramble,
'Til the butcher cut him down!

At the landing, a boat was making ready to leave.

An officer on the texas deck called out, 'Boy! You want a job?'

'Yes sir!' cried Lucky Al.

'Come aboard! We need a coal passer!'

Five days later, clad in long pants, Al was ranging the streets of Memphis, thinking of its pharaoh, the fabulous Boss Crump.

> Boss Crump don't 'low no long pants
> A-round here;
> Boss Crump don't 'low no long pants a-round here!
> I don't care what Crump don't 'low,
> Wear long pants any-how,
> Crump go out and get yourself some air.

And then Al and a salesman who'd picked him up hitchhiking, drank moonshine and talked about the big real-estate boom in Miami and invented verses for the Boss Crump Blues as they rolled along US 64 across plains, hills and mountains, on the way to Chattanooga. Al didn't show it, but he was scared, and sorry he'd set out into the unknown, alone. Being away from home the first time, away from familiar scenes, parents, friends, frightened him. He'd set out on the fateful journey of Everyman. And now, he's done it again, but this time he can't come back. No way!

'Goddamnit Bill, you've got it all wrong.'

It *had* to be like that.

'Bill, I never should have endowed my stool.'

Why not?

'You don't deserve it.'

Want me to finish the ocean burial? Flush the remains of your cremains down the toilet?

'I should have had them plant me in a cemetery with my golf clubs and credit cards and my fortune in gold coins and booby-trapped the hell out of it and covered it with cement.'

> What tale do you tell, Billy Boy, Billy Boy?
> What do you say of Al, charming Billy?
> Al's plunging into strife,
> Endangering his life,

DEAD AL

He's a young lad, and should not leave
His mother.

That damned Chorus is always on your side, Al.

'Okay, Bill, here's what really happened. No sooner had I shown my thumb down there in Memphis than a pea-green, disc-wheeled Dodge sedan stopped. The driver, a fat man in a checkered cap, smiled and waved me in. On the back seat lay some catalogs and a copy of *Mortuary Management* magazine. He wore checkered knickerbockers too.

The car sang through the gears. 'My name's Charon von Styx. You can call me Charley.'

'Thanks for the ride, Charley.'

'So what's your name, son?'

'Tross. Al B. Tross.'

'I'll bet you're wondering what I do for a living.'

'What do you do?'

'I sell Polish polish.'

'You're kidding!'

'Would I kid an albatross?'

'Would I accept a ride from Charon?'

We erupted into roars of mirth.

'So what do *you* do, Al?'

'I'm an adventurous traveler.'

'Me, Al, what I *really* do is administer cures for sales resistance.' He reached back into a wooden case and plucked out a Coke. He opened it, spilled some out the window, poured in white lightning from another Coke bottle, and toasted me. 'Al, I serve mankind as a Memorial Counselor. Which is to say I go around Tennessee selling graveyard plots. Pre-need, you know. At-need and post-need too, if I can. I hope that doesn't diminish me in your esteem.'

'My pa told me to respect gray hairs, even on a dog.'

We screamed and whooped with laughter. I raised the Coke to him and sang:

*'Ever' time I come to town
The boys keep kickin' my dog aroun';
Don't make no difference if he is a houn',
They gotta quit kickin' my dog aroun'!'*

Now we're getting the tone of it, Bill. I should have told
Charley I'm a moron. An oxy-moron, cynical but trusting.
After all, trust is what holds it all together. I keep my promises,
too. That way it's easier to say no. I left Charley in
Chattanooga early on a Saturday morning, mid-July, jungle
weather, sweating like a horse in Hell. I caught a train to
Dayton and spent the hour it took to get there daydreaming
and reading the *Chattanooga News*: RAULSTON
BANS DEFENSE EXPERTS; DARROW INSULTS
COURT. I'd already missed five days of the trial! The final
session, the paper thought, would be on Monday. We clacked
along between blue-gray mountain ridges up the Tennessee
River Valley into what Charley had called Sergeant York
country. Sergeant York, you'll recall, raised himself to glory
by killing two hundred and thirty-four Germans, all by himself. The Civil War left a leopard skin of blue and gray
death-spots spread over this valley, a pall even bloodier than
the one it spread over my home turf: Red-Leg Jayhawker
Dalton Quantrell Jesse James 'Little Dixie' western Missouri.
My forebears, all Rebels or children of Rebels, fed me their
blood stories along with my baby milk. Likewise, doubtless,
with the folks around here. Because it kept Missouri in the
Union, my pa liked to say the Yankee victory in the First
Battle of Boonville saved the United States and decided the
future history of the world. 'Even so, son, had I been alive in
those days, you'd have found me with General Lee.' Our
family springs from the Kentucky and Virginia folk who
settled our town. Loyal to slavery, this bogus gentry organized
the Thespian Society, and, helped by slaves, built Thespian
Hall, an impressive neo-classical theater building with two-
story brick columns in front. Life-loving slavery-hating
Germans composed Boonville's other magnetic pole. They
belonged to the Turnverein, an athletic and singing society

established in Germany to resist the Napoleonic occupation. Thespian or Turner? South pole or north pole? What would *I* have done in sixty-one? When walking around downtown, every time I passed the jail, a stone jail, and noticed it, I cringed. Not because I feared sheriffs or arrest, but because my mind's eye focussed on the slaves building it. Slavery sickened Mark Twain, too.

Thespian or Turner?

On which side would I have fought?

Rebel or Yankee?

Since childhood this riddle had produced day-and-night-mares and dreams. As I looked out the train window at the Tennessee Valley rushing by I scanned the features of the Confederate and Union troops we passed, seeking my face, and finding it in both armies. Harry Truman, a son of slave-owners and Rebels, scorned the Dixiecrats and their racist electoral votes. Harry Truman integrated the armed forces, just as seamen had integrated the National Maritime Union a decade earlier. Thespian or Turner? Truman's grandfather was a wagonmaster taking settlers west on the Santa Fe Trail, and Truman, before he turned eighteen, had read every book in the Independence library. Whose army would *he* have joined? How about me? Maybe, like Mark Twain, I would have shunned them both and lit out for the Territories.

I plunged back into the newspaper. Judge Raulston had ruled the Scopes defense could not put their scientific experts on the witness stand. Just before adjourning his court for the weekend, the judge, a Baptist from Fiery Gizzard, Tennessee, in response to Darrow's disdainful remarks, said, 'I hope you do not mean to reflect upon the court.'

'Well, your honor has the right to hope.'

I had missed all the fun.

The train slowed through the business district to stop at the station.

Well, maybe not *all*.

Alighting in this town of two thousand, I found myself caught up in a throng of shirtless, sunburned farmers in bib-overalls and wide-brimmed straw hats; city gents, coatless, in crisp boaters; lads my age still in knickers and shorts; blacks; dirty children; preachers in reversed collars; horses in canvas collars; mules in straw hats; mud-splattered Model-T's, mostly open with cloth tops like the numerous buggies they resembled. Up under the shady maple trees on the main street – Main Street – and in the yards on Market Street and on back streets as well, the men and boys, women and girls, as thick as hasty pudding, circulated under flags and banners and streamers and washing and monkey pennants as they moved by the markets and the two banks and Robinson's Drug Store and the library and Fischer's Ice Cream Parlor and the grammar school now serving as a cafeteria and the town's nine churches and the Hotel Aqua. And they swarmed on the courthouse lawn around a barbecue pit and over bleachers erected before a yellow-pine platform whence a Flat Earth Christian implored brethren and sistren to prepare for Judgment and condemned both Darrow and Bryan as infidels for denying the Bible's conception of the earth as flat. On the lawn and on Main and on Market stood hundreds of folding chairs along with public outhouses, hot-dog and lemonade stands, tent shows, fortune tellers. Fiddlers sawed, banjoers picked and thumbed, strongmen struggled to raise weights. Hooded photographers worked behind tripods and families snapped the scene with their Brownies. Down at the river, primitive Christians wallowed shouting praises to the Lord while an organ grinder and his monkey performed on the bank.

Everywhere, folks sucked Coca-Cola bottles, gulped moon-shine, devoured watermelons, licked ice cream. Posters depicting monkeys with coconuts embellished shop windows. Robinson's Drug Store, the town's social center, offered Monkey Fizzes at its soda fountain. In Robinson's and in booths and stands outside, merchants displayed monkey dolls, wind-up monkeys, monkey postcards, monkey watch fobs, monkey cookies, buttons saying YOUR OLD MAN'S A MONKEY, and even yet more bizarre and arcane instruments devised for extracting the last ounce of money out of *monkey*.

And in the Anti-Evolution League's bookstalls: *Hell and the High Schools; Evolution or Christ?; God or Gorilla?* And Bryan's own, *In His Image*.

And on the butcher shop: WE HANDLE ALL MEATS BUT MONKEY.

And on J. R. Darwin's Everything-to-Wear Store, a gigantic banner: DARWIN IS RIGHT – inside.

And out in a pasture Curtis Jennies flying in newspapers and flying out photographic plates.

And on Main Street the bibble Bible babble of glossolalia: folks possessed by Odun and Legba speaking in tongues.

And hot! Hotter than the bluest gridiron in the fire box of Hell.

And through this cacophonic chaos, by means of a tiller, an elderly dowager guided a stately dark-blue electric car.

> *Boiling cabbage down down*
> *Turn the hoe-cake round round,*
> *The onliest song I can sing*
> *Is boiling cabbage down!*

Chorus! You've got it wrong! You're worse than Bill. The locals, although mainly devout Christians – Adamists – were friendly and courteous and civilized and delighted to see Dayton, Tennessee, putting itself on the map along with the Wright Brothers' Dayton, Ohio, and the Army Camel Corps' Dayton, Nevada.

But as for the visitors! That's a different story. They'd emerged from the pages of *Weird Tales* magazine offered for sale on Robinson's rack.

A showman paraded an ape clad in a suit, shirt, tie, hat, shoes, spats. The ape brandished a walking stick.

Another showman exhibited Big Joe, an adult chimpanzee, and Little Joe, a microcephalic midget from Burlington, Vermont.

A flapper – masculine haircut, short skirt, stockings rolled below the knees – stepped out of a yellow roadster.

A baby lay in its carriage teething on a cap pistol.

An old man in a ragged army shirt offered for sale a monkey head with antlers – goat antlers.

Two boys struggled in the dust for possession of a broken stick of striped candy.

From the doorway of a cabin on wheels a clergyman from Georgia, clad in a top hat, alpaca coat, police pants, preached against blacks.

Newsmen greeted colleagues: Brother, thy tail hangs down behind, thus eliciting: Thy tail hangs down behind, Brother.

An ancient bearded prophet seized my hand and said, 'I am John the Baptist the Third. No good can come of this. The children of God will still believe in the Bible. The children of man will still follow evolution. It is all useless. It should stop. I am commanded to bid it stop.'

And a sign-toting primitive paused before me to make sure I read his message:

> The Kingdom of God, Paradise Street, is at hand.
> Forty Days of Prayer itemizing your sins and iniquities
>   for eternal life – if you come clean.
> God will talk back to you in voice.
> Deck Carter
Bible Champion of the World.

And a preacher declaiming from a table top spied me and called down, 'Boy! The mark of the Beast is on the people of this town and the Devil's got them, sure as anything. Yes, Satan has Darrow and Scopes, and, son, you too. I can see it in your eyes.'

'The Beast?'

'Yes! With seven heads and ten horns! All this talk about monkeys shows the mark of the beast on this wicked town. You'll all be cast down into the Lake of Fire!'

I caught sight of a big man in a panama hat, a bundle of fresh vegetables under one arm, walking toward the dining room of the Aqua.

That's Bryan.

And then I spied Darrow's entourage standing on the tiled floor of Robinson's Drug Store surrounding a man reclining in a chair by a soda-fountain table, sipping a malted milk. Clarence Darrow!

Bryan was taller then me, Darrow somewhat shorter. Both had big heads and were about as elegant as a dog eating breakfast. Bryan! Thrice nominated for president by the Democratic Party, my party. And Darrow, like Bryan, a legend, like Bryan, a champion of the common man. In court, Darrow had called Bryan foolish, wicked, and malevolent. Darrow, with no help from Upstairs, defended the outcast, the outlaw, the free thinker. I felt great sympathy for this slovenly old man who defied public opinion and revealed religion in the interests of intellectual liberty, and I still do.

Over on the courthouse lawn, in the shade of ancient maple trees with whitewashed trunks, Bryan was about to speak. Before the platform sat a telegrapher who would transmit the proceedings for broadcast on WGN, Chicago. Munching a radish drawn from his pocket, Bryan mounted the platform. The loudspeakers attached to the courthouse façade were on but he would scorn them for he was said to have the loudest mellowest voice in the whole fucking world. He stood there, cooling himself with a palmleaf fan presented by a local undertaker, waiting for the cheers and applause to subside. He'd rolled up his sleeves and turned his shirt collar under. A train whistle cut through the cries of his enthusiasts. Bryan seemed to me a big, old man, bald and benign, my grandfather, our family doctor.

Transformed suddenly into an evangel of the Lord, he raised both hands high, then began to speak.

In a powerful, hypnotic voice not unlike Adolf Hitler's, he told of the people's right to decide what should and should not be taught in public schools. 'The hand that writes the paycheck should rule the school.' He spoke of an Armageddon joined here in Dayton where the forces of the Lord would prevail over the dark legions of Satan. He called Darrow a

SQUED

heretic, an infidel. 'Instead of doing Great God's good, that man uses his marvelous gifts as fangs to tear at the breast of Christianity.'

Eardrum-crushing cheers and applause.

A horizontal gesture of his hands hushed to silence.

'*Evil*-ution is the doctrine of the Devil. What care I for the age of rocks when I stand upon the Rock of Ages!'

This produced a tremendous ovation. He had finished. I walked away. His crusade for Prohibition had mutated the Constitution. Could his crusade for the literal acceptance of Bible babble do the same? Blanket roll slung, I hiked out to Monkey House, the mansion in the country where the defense had its headquarters. The Lord had sent Bryan to earth to lead men back to the true faith. As with Mohammed, his every word came from God. He could do no wrong. He was righteousness embodied. He preached the social Gospel. The hearts of the people, inspired by God, like Bryan himself, cannot be wrong. As few others in the public eye have done, he had spent his life fighting for the common man. Simple people loved and trusted him. He seemed absolutely honest. He was a Democrat and a democrat. He had no sense of humor. He was ignorant beyond belief. He knew less about science than a pig knows about algebra. Like consuls of ancient Rome, he and his colleague, Darrow, presided over this allegory, this parable, this American pageant we still remember in 1990; he, a Bugs Bunny forever munching radishes, a legendary glutton, endlessly gorging on gigantic breakfasts, mammoth luncheons, enormous dinners.

At the Monkey House folks told me I could use their water and their privy.

While picnicking on the lawn I caught sight of Scopes, who, people said, hid when not in court. Scopes. A slender young man with reddish hair and glasses, twenty-four but younger looking. Scopes. A man whom I, an only child, would welcome as my big brother.

Early Sunday morning I awoke and walked back to town. There I met some sports from Saint Louis who had heard of my grandfather. I accepted their invitation to drive up into the mountains where, concealed, they were going to watch a Holy Roller Sabbath service. Monday morning found me on the ravaged courthouse lawn, one of a throng, looking at the red-brick building and its squat clock-tower crowned with a white cupola, listening to the procedings broadcast by loudspeakers.

Judge Raulston ruled Darrow in contempt of court for the contempt he'd shown Friday. At the opening of the afternoon session, Darrow said on reading the transcript over the week-end he'd concluded he'd been wrong and, rather sullenly, he apologized. In the name of Christian mercy, Judge Raulston forgave him. Then, remembering, perhaps, the Virginia Supreme Court had once fallen through a floor of the Capitol on to the heads of the legislature, and deeming his own court-house floor too weak for the safety of the crowd, Judge Raulston ordered the trial moved outside on to the lawn.

Up went a tremendous cry of joy.

Presently, functionaries and volunteers swarmed over the platform with chairs and tables and typewriters and other essentials. People made benches from planks, brought chairs and crates from their houses, clambered to the tops of cars parked by the curb while boys scaled the gigantic maple shading the platform. Once the stage was set, the actors took their places.

The judge called for the jury.

A ten-foot sign saying READ YOUR BIBLE would be visible to the jury. Darrow demanded it be removed or else be accompanied by another: READ YOUR EVOLUTION.

Judge Raulston ordered it removed.

Then a defense lawyer called a Bible expert – Bryan himself – to the stand. Despite objections from his own colleagues, Bryan agreed to witness. At last the two champions, one of revelation, one of science, would meet face to face.

Bryan, coatless, in striped pants and a stiff, white shirt with black bow tie, sat on an office swivel chair. Calmly fanning, he gazed at his mortal enemy.

Darrow slouched over him, thin graying hair, lined face, blue shirt and blue suspenders, pockets stuffed with papers.

'You have given considerable study to the Bible, haven't you Mr Bryan?'

For what seemed like hours, Darrow paced, drooped then snapped his head up to speak, stood bent, arms folded, or tapped his gold-rimmed glasses against his sleeve, or rocked, thumbs hooked on his suspenders. Sometimes he reclined against the rail, and sometimes his whole body shrugged infinite contempt, suggesting boundless reserves of power as yet unused. And all the while, traversing cloudbursts of objections, he stabbed and lashed Bryan with questions aimed at contradictions within the Bible and between the Bible and the vast knowledge of science. Had Jonah really lived inside a fish? Was the fish made especially for the purpose? Did Joshua make the sun stand still to lengthen the day? Or was it really the earth he arrested? Did the snake walk on his tail before he was cursed to go on his belly? Did God make woman out of a rib or out of dust? Where did Cain get his wife? Were Egyptian and Chinese civilizations here before The Flood? How old is civilization, anyway? How old is the world? What, before God created the sun and the moon, was the nature of the days and nights mentioned in Genesis? How long were they? Were all objects and forms of life, and all civilization too, created during and after 4004 BC?

Save for what's in the Bible – and even there his knowledge was defective – Bryan neither knew nor wished to know about these and other matters, matters he'd pontificated upon for years.

'I do not think about the things I don't think about.'

'Do you think about the things you *do* think about?'

'Well, sometimes.'

The audience swung away from him. He was being humbled and humiliated before those who adored him.

Finally, both men were on their feet, shaking fists. Bryan turned to the people and cried out that Darrow's only purpose was to *slur the Bible*.

'I object to your statement! I am examining you on your fool ideas no intelligent Christian on earth believes!'

Judge Raulston stopped the fight by adjourning the court,

quite possibly thereby averting a riot. Bryan sagged into his chair. 'Slurring the Bible . . . slurring the Bible . . . '

The decision went to Darrow by a TKO.

Orgasm over, emotion subsided, spent. I overheard Darrow say to a comrade, 'Rusting in the heart of every evangelist lies the wreck of a confidence man.'

The next day the Louisville *Courier-Journal* headlined: 3,000 AT APE TRIAL GET THRILL. For reasons of appeal, and to frustrate a Bryan summation, Darrow asked the jury to return a verdict of guilty. They did so in eight minutes. Raulston fined Scopes one hundred dollars. Visitors began leaving town. I found work on a clean-up crew. Sunday, Bryan ate his usual enormous dinner, then, napping, he died in his sleep.

Darrow said to friends, 'Now, wasn't that man a God-damned fool?'

H. L. Mencken said to the world, 'Well, we killed the son-of-a-bitch.'

As for me, although all along I felt sorry for him, I say, 'Amen!'

FIVE

Eight hundred miles and two weeks later I stepped off the train. Home at last. But Dayton had followed me. It was as if I'd never left there. The first thing I saw outside the station was a florid man standing in a wagon preaching at a bored mule who was hitched to it and at a number of folks who weren't. Nailed to the wagon, a banner: TAKE THE EVIL OUT OF BOONEVILLE.

'Boy, you come here.'

I felt like saying, Look at me, long pants; you can't call me boy any more. But I didn't. I went over to join his flock.

'Boy, you done got off that train in an evil town. There's evil in the D*evil*, evil in the *evil*ution they teach here in school, and evil in Booneville. Join me, brother, and take the evil *out*.'

'Brother,' I replied in a loud voice, 'there ain't no evil *in* Boonville. You spelled it wrong.'

He raised his hands, embracing us all, the mule too, although, as I wanted to say, soul-less, the mule was out of the game.

'Brothers and sisters, I'm here to testify, with the joy of God in my heart, that Hell is hot, Heaven is sweet, Judgment is sure, Jesus saves, and the Bible is true.' He pointed at me. 'Boy, are you with Jesus?'

'No. He stayed aboard and rode on to Kansas City.' I decided I'd better be cautious. 'Praise the Lord!' I cried out.

I crossed the street. 'Al! *Al!*' It was my friend, Tommy. 'You just get in?'

'Sure did.' I put my arm around his shoulder. Pals could do that in those days. 'I'll walk you home,' he said.

I told him about leaving Jesus on the train.
'Folks been wondering about you. Where you been?'
'The Monkey Trial.'
'Honest Injun?'
'Honest Injun.'
We walked to the river and then along Water Street by brick warehouses and steamboats to the new bridge. We paused to watch the cars through the metal grating of their roadway overhead, and when they passed over it, it trembled and said ttnnnnnng. As we ascended the Main Street grade to the business district Tommy told me he'd followed the Monkey Trial in the papers and, he guessed, so had everyone else. 'And they're really hot about it, believe me, they are!'

> Jesus, he died on Cal-ga-ry Street,
> Nails in his hands and
> Nails in his feet,
> He was somebody's lov-er,
> Somebody's son,
> Yet they left him to die . . . there
> Like an old drunken bum.

Did I sing that, or was it the Chorus?
'Tell me about it, Al, the Monkey Trial. Tell me all about it.'
I didn't have my own mind made up about it yet. I knew he'd want me to tell him what to think. It had been, all at once, a state fair, a political campaign, a church picnic, and more. We turned into High Street. I decided here at home all I'd tell people was the funny part. For the rest, they could rely on the papers. I'd fill them in on John the Baptist III and the Bible Champion of the World. The first thing I told Tommy was about me and those sports from Saint Louis spying on the Holy Rollers. It made us laugh, but I felt guilty, too, telling it the way I told it, because in those days, before radio made a single city out of the whole world, life in the mountains was even harder than it is now and, especially for women, there was very little to do except drudge and suffer.

'At dusk, Tommy, we crept up on them through a cornfield, like hunters after snipe.' They'd gathered around a big old oak tree and were sitting on benches and on the ground. In the light of torches flaring from a low limb you could see their faces and, right in the middle, their leader, bib-overalls, round eye-glasses, shirt open showing more hair than his head did. He began pacing under the flames, preaching, and at each turn he flung his arms aloft and yelled out, Glorrrrry be to God!

He was carrying on about how on the Day of Judgment the high kings of the world, especially the King of Greece-y, would fall over and die and slide right down to Hell, and believe me, we were quiet as anything, because if they saw us we'd be about as welcome as prickly heat on a bride's crotch. Yea and verily, brothers and sisters, he was booming, on the Great Day all the high and mighty, those prideful, blasphemous servants of Beelzebub and Satan, rotten through with sin, will be flung down into the eternal torments of Hell while we saints are walking up the rocky road to Heaven.

The crowd was swaying back and forth to his rhythm and shouting A-men and just as I'd begun thinking these people are the world's best argument for birth control a skinny woman, her gray hair drawn into a bun, rose to denounce books, all but the Bible, for if a book's true everything in it's already in the Bible, and if it's false, reading it will give you gangrene of the soul.

Next, a farmer in a straw hat testified that speaking in tongues is real, schools are a snare, and as soon as his children get so they can read the Bible they'll have had plenty of schooling. More will lead them to damnation! A fat man in a derby hat rises up and says sin is everywhere and Dayton is worse than Sodom. And the stringy woman stands and yells out Praise the Lord and soon she's leaping and shrieking and they start singing hymns and the last hymn goes on and on and changes into a monotonous chant, and they're all beating time, and men move a bench to the brightest spot beneath the flickering flaming torches.

A nice looking yellow-haired girl comes out of the shadows and lies down on it.

The leader motions for silence.

'This sister has asked for prayers.'

He signals and they all, every one of them, crowd up to the bench and begin to pray, not together but each for himself. Another signal: they all fall to their knees and thrust their arms out over her. The boss is kneeling facing our way and he keeps tossing his head and taking it in his hands and words rip out of him defying the imps and demons of the air and imploring God to pull the girl back out of Hell. And he stands and looks at the stars and begins to babble in tongues and his voice rises higher and higher and finally shrills out a hideous squawk and some of them flop right down on top of her and he lies down on them. And a woman in a homemade cap pulls herself out of the heap and her veins are swollen and her fists are at her throat and she bends way back and snaps forward and begins to convulse in some kind of fit. And more women detach themselves from the heap and flip into frenzied fits and couples are going off together into the corn and I keep seeing flashes of the girl's yellow hair and I throw myself right on to that pile and roll around with the rest of them deep in the stink of sweat and crusty assholes.

By now those Saint Louie sports are so scared and pale you could make black marks on them with chalk. So they drag me off the pile and we get the hell out of there.

Tommy was wide-eyed impressed, proud to be seen with me, and ashamed of his short pants, him being four months older than me. 'Gee, Al, is that all you took with you, just the blanket roll?'

'Yep.'

'What would you have done if it rained?'

'Got wet.'

We came to four steps leading into a little park and I paused to smile at them. They never failed to amuse me. In a white triangle at their base, red and green mosaic letters spelled out: BELL'S VIEW PARK. At this moment was old Bell, the Apple King of Missouri, viewing us from his house across the street? The steps were made of hideous, sandy gray concrete. Large Roman letters impressed into the top step declared: GET BUSY, STAY BUSY: AVOID WASTE, VICE, TOBACCO, BOOZE: AND YOU WILL HAVE HEALTH. HONOR AND PLENTY. C.C.B.

We crossed thirty feet of lawn to the bottom of the park and sat on the stone wall there overlooking the wide Missouri. Kicking our heels, we watched the tugs and barges and steamboats riding on its sunbright yellow surface.

'Tell me about Bryan and Darrow.'

'I'm not going to talk about them, Tommy. I'm not going to talk about the serious side at all, not until I get the whole thing straight in my head, and maybe not even then.'

'Come on, you can tell *me*.'

'Old pal, when I get ready to tell, I'll tell you first. I've got my reasons for keeping my mouth shut. You know me as well – better, than anybody. You know I want to keep on being popular in this town. I'm going to be valedictorian at school. I'm going to earn my football letter. Then I'll go down to Columbia to law school just like my pa, and then I'll come back and make big money and go into politics.'

Tommy, beaming at me, hit my shoulder. 'And if I ever get in a jam, I'll know who to call up.'

I said goodbye and walked up Eighth toward home, a modern brick house on the corner of Morgan. I walked right in. My mother greeted me with a whoop and a kiss, pa smiled a big happy smile and, accepting my hand, gave me his best hand-crushing shake.

It worked out just as I'd planned. By the end of summer I was more popular than ever and nobody knew what I really thought about things. Pa had accepted my long pants. All the girls loved me. Working at the landing put money in my pocket. I had my eye on buying a lovely green Essex roadster. The principal, of all things a member of the World Christian Fundamentals Association, told me he planned to hold an assembly on the first day of school and expected me, as student body president, to address it. That would really be fun. I trusted the principal. Why not? In those days I believed the authorities worthy of their authority, even President Coolidge. If they were not awesomely deserving, the other adults would not trust them with awesome powers. They must have a manlier, a deeper, wisdom than I did. They were right even when I thought them wrong, right even when my pride made me stand against them. The principal seemed smooth and confident, and friendly too, so I didn't worry about his fundamentalist tendencies. After all, private life is not public life.

But as it turned out, the principal was too selfish to respect the difference. You know, a good Christian – scared of life, scared of death, scared of the sequel.

When my pa dropped me off at Main and Locust to go into the school and backstage in the auditorium I shone with high spirits. Ever since the principal had told me he expected me to speak I'd been thinking about what I would say and how I would say it. I'd perfected my speech, memorized it, and, rehearsing gestures and expressions, I'd delivered it time after time to my mirror. My speech was short, perfect. Its theme was an old saying about the wagons that used to go in convoys from Independence to Oregon and California. 'The timid never started, the weak died on the way.' Many of those wagons had come through Boonville en route to Independence. The wagon trip represented a golden future possible for us all. Here in school, as of now, we resolve to devote ourselves to preparing for the trip. We will strengthen our characters, we will define our destinations and our routes, we will learn as much as we can and thus improve our chances for success. If in this way we give ourselves the best chance for success, and nonetheless we fail, we will be the stronger for having tried. At this point I'd talk about our football team. Dare to try for success. No matter what, do your best. When the going gets tough, the tough get going. No pain, no gain. Yes. My speech would grab them all by the short hairs.

The principal, a bearlike man with a bear's voice, led us class officers from the wings onto the stage. We seated ourselves in a line of chairs behind the rostrum. I spied Tommy in the front row and winked at him. Persisting with my benign smile, I gazed from face to face. The principal stepped to the lectern.

'I welcome you to a challenging new school year, one which opens the second quarter of our century. When you arrive at mid-century your children will be seated here, listening to another principal, and you will be conducting the affairs of our town, perhaps of our state, or even our nation. Of those of us who are doing so now, many will have returned to dust, and their souls will be receiving their just rewards. So here, at once, you are preparing yourselves for two futures. For the future of adult responsibility. And for the future of eternal life in Heaven, or, God forbid, in Hell. Here in school you prepare yourselves for life before, and even more important, *after* death. For we Christians, death is not the end of life. No. Death is the *beginning*. Death, young friends, is *birth*!'

He beamed down on the audience.

'In July, in Dayton, Tennessee, an allegory – a parable – unrolled before the eyes of the world. In it we saw the clash of the profane and the divine, of faith in man and faith in God. In what seemed to be a triumph of Satan, the great and noble William Jennings Bryan achieved martyrhood. I pledge to you, and to our families and our town, the forces that possessed Darrow and killed Bryan will neither possess nor kill you. Here in our school, the divine as expressed in the Bible will be our guide. Young friends, we do not see science standing in opposition to religion, demanding of us a choice. No. Science *is* religion. All science consists with the words of the Bible, of the Lord Who created it along with everything else. The Lord's science is the light guiding us into the second quarter of this century. The Bible will lead us into a warless world where all men are brothers, where all men prosper in Christian dignity. Your work here is God's work. From here you will go on to create a better future on earth for all, and, in Heaven, for yourself.'

Tommy's features expressed the thoughtful silence of the auditors. Then came a wave of applause. The principal remained standing, solemn, until it hushed.

'Young friends. It is now my privilege to present the elected spokesman of your generation, of those who, at mid-century, will be conducting our affairs. I know he, too, will urge you to follow the Lord's way. I give you your president, Alvin Burke.'

Sweating like a whore in church, I mounted the rostrum.

My forearms on the lectern, I scanned the faces.

Tommy and the rest expressed trust, an utter openness to whatever I would choose to present.

'Brothers and sisters. In the second quarter of the last century, when drawn by dreams of a better life on the Pacific Coast people began crossing the prairies and mountains in their wagons, folks around here used to say, "The timid never started, the weak died on the way." Today, our football coach tells us, "When the going gets tough, the tough get going."'

Moving along from there I rendered my wagonmaster football-coach speech perfectly. Tommy looked convinced but disappointed. The teachers were mainly smiling. But then, and it was as if I were hovering in the air, listening, looking down at myself speak, not knowing what would come next, I heard myself say, 'You've all been asking me about creation and evolution, about Bryan and Darrow, and I've been telling you funny stories about the carnival part of what happened in Dayton, but nothing about the serious part and what I think about it.'

Stiffening, my voice surged on.

'Darrow believes in a slow development of the earth and of life on it over millions, if not billions, of years. Darrow's view is supported by all the evidence, by people's observations added up and compared. Bryan believed in creation in six days. If he'd had his way, that and only that would be taught in our school. He also believed Jonah lived inside a fish. He believed Jacob climbed to Heaven on a firemen's ladder. He believed a man could walk on water. He believed the Red Sea drew itself back to form a path for an army to cross. He believed a woman could turn into a pillar of salt. He believed Cain's wife came from nowhere. He believed Joshua made the sun stand still. That, of course, means the sun goes around the earth. But Bryan was a hypocrite. He waffled that and he denied the earth is flat even though flat-earth Christians can and do give ample Bible references to prove it.

'If they have their way about teaching six-day creation and nothing else here in our school, to be honest they must teach all the rest and nothing else. They must teach all those other Truths and only them. They will repeal the law of gravity, regulate the speed of light, and expel those of us who say the earth is round.

'Bryan knows less about science than a hog knows about the Bible.

'Reason killed Bryan. Oppose his resurrection!

'Darrow is *right*.'

Suddenly once more inside of myself, using Bryan's horizontal gesture, I hushed the non-existent applause. I assumed a dramatic Bryanesque pose.

'What care I for the Rock of Ages when I stand upon the Age of Rocks!' I declaimed in my most resonant voice.

In arctic silence I sat down.

The principal strode to the lectern. He stood mute until he gained our absolute attention.

'Boonville is a Christian community. An infidel cannot represent its youth and its children in any capacity. Consequently, I declare the student body election of June tenth null-and-void and the position of student body president vacant. I order that that vacancy be filled in an election to be held two weeks from today.'

He paused.

'Assembly dismissed.'

He came over to me where, crushed, I sat.

He spoke to me quietly, in a kind voice.

'You go now, son.'

I went. I didn't stop until I got to New Orleans, and didn't stop then, because as a result of the boom, and my good luck, I found work as an ordinary seaman on a ship bound for the Mediterranean: The Romance Run. I finally came to a halt in bed with a black-haired sporting girl in a whorehouse in the Gothic Quarter of Barcelona.

SIX

I remember sitting here a few years ago, Al and me, by ourselves, drinking after hours, Jack Daniels on the rocks, just as I am now, and Al's saying in that smooth voice of his – like the rest of him it seems untouched by age – he's saying, 'Now that I'm approaching eighty, every morning when I get up and go to my window to shut it, I pause to look out over the rooftops at the ocean. I sometimes spit down into my garden and I breathe that good California air, thinking, Well, Al, here comes another day. In that thought is a wonder, a gratitude, a resolve that because it may be my last, I'll make the most of it.

'The feeling's not new for me. I felt that way sailing cargo ships during the war. We were always aware submarines moved down there in the deep and might sink us at any moment without warning. Up here with the Alives, and then *boom*, down there with the Deads.' He snapped his fingers. 'Just like *that*. You'd be dozing warm and comfortable in your bunk, or eating steak and eggs in the mess-room, or standing at the wheel up on the bridge watching the bow rise and smash down in a fan of spray, and then abruptly find yourself in cold water, swimming, watching ships go by and vanish because convoys never stopped. And, especially if you'd been on a tanker, you might find yourself swimming in flaming oil. That nightmare always lay there just under awareness and rose up in dreams or maybe in a nervous panic during the solitude of lookout. After it happened to me, I could not put it out of my head. No oil, but dark and stormy and cold and seven hundred miles from shore. I caught a life ring thrown to me off a Liberty ship. As a result of her forward motion the line attached to the ring pulled me alongside. They dropped a ladder. Talk about good luck! That's why I'm sitting here now. Out there, each new day was a handful of gold. And a week or two on shore: Party time! We thought the war would never end. I kept going back, although I really didn't have to. I made myself go back because I owed it to my union brothers and my friends, to America. You know, it's a fact. All those years I lived with the certainty sooner or later the war would eat me.'

He was pensively swirling the ice in his glass.

'On the Murmansk Run, you know, up into the Arctic Sea to the Soviet Union, that feeling intensified to some kind of ultimate. Going out and coming back, it peaked in the dead space between the farthest range of our fighter planes and those of the Soviets. German U-boats and planes used to take out forty, fifty percent of a convoy, sink the ships in water so cold you could not live in it. Like with atom war, survivors did not survive.'

The German captains and pilots never chose the ships Lucky Al sailed on, not in those waters. They caught him that one time in the Atlantic and, once again, in summer, in the Med.

They chose not to break his chain of days.

Nor had anyone else or anything else, not until two weeks ago.

Two weeks ago he entered entropy.

'What's it like there on the Other Side?'

The Chorus is singing *Kindertotenlieder* – child-death songs.

During the war I was an adolescent, healthy and athletic, and if anyone was ever set to feel immortal, it should have been me. I went to basic training and then spent the rest of the war fighting the Battles of Saint Louis, Peoria, and Chicago, gathering in free drinks and friendly ladies. I was never in danger. None the less, I had the same feeling Al did. And so, I think, did most of the rest of the twelve million in our armed forces, and the Canadians, and the Soviets, and the Aussies, and the Brits, and maybe even the Japanese and Germans, though they thought they were going to win. Just like Al, I knew the war would go on for ever and ever and eventually it would eat me.

I know exactly how he felt. I know his life as if it were mine. Death waits everywhere. That, as Al liked to say, is life.

But that's only the personal dimension. 'World War II,' said Al, 'the Soviets call it the Great Patriotic War. You know, most people – young people especially, but not Billy, because I've told him about it often enough – most people don't know how close it was. We almost *lost* that war. People forget the Germans ruled Europe and North Africa, the Japanese controlled all of East Asia. Both the Germans and the Japanese were mobilizing immense populations as slave labor for arms manufacture, as military recruits, as scientists and technicians devoted to making better weapons. We stood against the power of two continents. By 1945 the Germans had missiles and jet planes, by 1947 they would have had the A-bomb! In 1940, the United Kingdom fought all alone! Churchill and King George VI had a machine-gun bunker built in front of Buckingham Palace. The two of them, the king and the prime minister, resolved to defend it to the death should the Germans get that far.

'We almost *lost* the Great Patriotic War. Believe me, it was close. Our victory gave civilization one more chance, its last, and that's where we are now.'

About a year after I met Al, I was driving back here across country from my mother's house in Chicago. Just before dark I picked up two young sailors hitch-hiking to Denver. I planned to drive straight through to Denver and hoped their conversation would keep me awake. About midnight they told me they were exhausted and asked if they could sleep in the back seat. Naturally I said yes, and soon they were curled up under their pea coats, invisible on this black black misty night. As my lights burned the way mile after mile through solid darkness from Iowa into Nebraska I began to feel a chill foreboding which I ascribed to my growing tendency to nod off to sleep. In a dark dead hamlet a man stood by the roadside, thumbing, and in hopes his company would help me stay awake, I stopped. A big and evil brute with jail tattoos and no baggage save his sullen and sinister air seated himself beside me. No cars or trucks at all seemed to be on the road that night. He told me he was going to Cheyenne and grunted a hostile *oh* when I said Cheyenne was out of my way. We hummed along for an endless silent time ever deeper into our tunnel of light. His menacing presence had aroused me more thoroughly than any conversation could have.

'Do you know who I am and why I'm here?' he said.

'No.'

He snapped on the dome light.

A revolver pointing at me gleamed in his left hand.

'I am Death. I am here to take you.'

I held a steady pressure on the accelerator.

A knife appeared in his right hand. He prodded my neck with it.

'First I'll cut your prick off and stuff it in your mouth.'

Slowly speeding up I tried to imagine what Al would do were he in my place.

'Then I'll shove this pistol up your ass and pull the trigger.'

Silent, I pressed the accelerator.

The knife point broke my skin.

'Slow down and stop.'

I maintained my speed.

Nothing whatever appeared in the tunnel of light.

On both sides stood bright walls of corn.

The knife turned against my flesh causing a sharp pain.

I pushed the horn ring producing a tremendous blare.

'Scared of Death ain't you.'

I kept on pushing the ring.

I did indeed feel myself in the presence of Death.

Abruptly, the sailors seized him from behind.

And gripping him in a choke hold, disarmed him.

I stopped the car and we pulled him out.

I told the boys to stop pounding him.

I held him at bay with the pistol.

What would Al do now?

DEAD AL

'Jack, you know what *I* did?'

I'm talking to Jack Daniels, imagining his face present on the bottle label.

'We made him strip, Jack, bare-ass totally. We left him there with nothing. Miles down the road we threw his wallet and knife and clothes and gun out into a cornfield.'

Did he learn his lesson?

'Violent crimes can often be traced to child abuse and, thence, to where child abuse comes from.'

'Ease off, Al. You know I don't converse with the dead.'

'I'll tell you some of *my* close call stories.'

'I've heard them all.'

'Not the new ones.'

'I'm against necromancy, and besides I don't believe in it.'

'I could tales unfold whose lightest words would harrow up thy young blood and cause thine eyes to start from their spheres like quills of fretful porpentine.'

'What's that?'

'Porcupine.'

'No stories, Al. Stop it, or . . . I'll dig you out of your squed and mix you with the stool stuffing.'

'You're not worthy of that stool.'

'I will be after I've stuffed it with your cremains. You'll get the farts and the wet pants first and can kiss ass to your heart's content.'

'I've a new motto for you and your place, Bill. *Poto, ergo sum*. Classical Latin for, I drink, therefore I am.'

> *It was down in old Bill's bar-room,*
> *On the road there by the sea,*
> *The drinks were served as us-u-al,*
> *And on Al's stool they'd soon be free.*

By means of the Saint James Infirmary Blues the Chorus was trying to tell me something. They'd acquired musical accompaniment.

From the radio behind the bar!

In came young Billy Will-i-ams,
He said: 'Old Al is dead!'
He gazed at us ranged before him,
'I wish it were me, instead.'

'Chorus! How can you be such sentimental assholes!'

'We *wish it were* you *instead.'*

The TV control's laying there in the tip gutter, right behind bottled Jack.

It's in my hand now.

I'll turn that fucking set on loud enough to blast that fucking Chorus right out of my place.

They went to the Neptune So-ci-e-ty,
They took old Alvin there;
Drove him out in Bill's blue Buick,
Left the five-ball, a lock of hair.

Loud! The TV snarls and snaps. My dish antenna reaches for Scotland. Harris tweed! Images now. Chorus, you're fired! I don't pay you, so this is the only way I can do it. You're eighty-sixed! That's what. *Do* it, TV – *do* it! Images are forming. The Close Call Show's over. Here's the Slovenly Peter Show. It's on *all* the channels. Blow that Chorus the fuck out . . . of . . . here! Tonight, seated in his nest of squalor and depravity, surrounded by paintings and bookcases stuffed with sado-porn, our host, Slovenly Peter, presents a rerun of The Story of Cruel Frederick: a naughty, nasty boy was he, much much worse than you and me. He caught up flies, poor simple things, and tore off their tiny wings. He killed the birds, and broke the chairs, and kicked his sister down the stairs; and oh! hear that bad boy curse as he atom-bombs the Universe! And then, oh then, I hate to say, we'll see him lash the gentle Tray. And kick the poor dog's dish away. And now, gedunk gedank, he hurls a ball against Tray's flank! The five-ball rolls across the floor while he-boy beats Tray more and more. Does good dog Tray sit up and beg? No, he bites the he-boy's leg! Cruel Frederick crawls away to bed; the Doctor comes and has him bled. And in Fred's place at the dinner table, Tray eats as much as he is able. The soup he swallows cup by cup; he chews the pies and puddings up! But does that teach the boy anything? Does Cruel Frederick learn his lesson? We hope so. But no! He thrusts pins through struggling butterflies, shoots birds and bees from out the skies; he smashes bugs with fearful blows, and all the time he grows and grows! He's a bully and a pervert, a boozer and a doper, a liar, a thief, a wifebeater, and as for Cruel Fredericks Two and Three? We shall see what we shall see.

Al always said old Enkidu and Winnetou, founders of the E & W Club, reminded him of lobster claws, the crusher and the ripper.

Maybe Slovenly Peter should produce an episode about them.

On the TV now, a commercial praising cheap cassettes of famous choirs.

This produces a furious quarrel between the TV and the Chorus.

The radio appeals to me for help against both of them.

'Get out of here, all of you! Leave me alone!'

SEVEN

Now I'm alone again and it's quiet.

Part of the story, part of it, about how we sent Al off to entropy, I've been holding back. Our physician friend came at once and, after a careful examination, pronounced Al dead. We drank a round of zombies astral to Al's fleeting spirit, and then another. We called the Neptune Society. They said they would cremate him as soon as he was delivered to them. Although we knew Al would forbid us to ship him there in an undertaker's hearse, Doc said we must proceed in a strictly legal fashion. Despite his retirement from practice, Doc could lawfully complete and sign the death certificate, which he did. He'd brought a blank along. Billy and I signed as witnesses. Then we flung Al's arms over our shoulders, pal-style, and walked him between us, feet dragging, down to my car, a classic Buick, a four-holer with a gleaming toothy grin. We placed him in the shotgun seat. In deference to law and to the absence of rigor mortis we secured his seat belt. Billy strapped himself in next to Al and I stretched Al's arm on top of the seat behind Billy and wedged it there. I closed the door. Al seemed to be dozing. Going around to my side I opened the door and spoke to Billy.

'Hang on there, I'll be right back.'

I trotted by some of Al's flowers up the front walk to the house. Inside, I paced through the rooms, seeking, but not sure what. I took the heirloom baseball off Billy's dresser, tossed it a few times, put it back. No. Billy would want to keep it for the next generation. Most of the stuff in Al's house except for books and furniture, I began to see, belonged to Billy. Al believed in living out of a seabag. A pilot chart of the South Pacific embellished the kitchen wall, and another, showing the arm and fist of Cape Cod, occupied a place where you could see it from the phone. Down in the game room I took the five-ball out of the rack and, grasping it, went back out to the car. I passed the ball to Billy and strapped myself in.

We drove up the street to Highway One and turned left, toward Frisco.

'You should have picked some of Al's flowers.'

'Al would want those flowers to stay there for the folks he left behind.' Besides that, he didn't want flowers associated with the disposal of his body. 'Old W. B. Antonelli, that prissy old mummy-maker, Al hated him about as much as he hated anybody, which wasn't much, used to load up all his funerals with flowers. Half the florist business's done with the dead. Makes funerals and weddings smell the same. Al didn't like that either.'

In my rearview I saw a highway patrol car. Billy gazed at the orange globe in his hand. 'Al told me pool is the golf of the poor.' Tanned, clad in shorts, he was hardly the companion you'd expect for a corpse. '*This*,' he said, displaying the ball, 'is Al's flower. Al said one reason he was so hot on pool is that his soul-father, Clarence Darrow, the lawyer he thought his father should have been, loved to play pool.' Billy put the ball in his back pocket. 'Funny thing, Al was fucking *old*. Yet I never called him anything but Al, and that always seemed natural.'

'I'm going to tell them to burn the ball along with him.'

For his last voyage, we'd dressed Al in an orange Welcome-Aboard-Yacht-*Ruby* sweatshirt. Billy had slipped on a dark blue *Ruby* T-shirt and a *Ruby* cap. He beamed at Dead Al, whose face we'd set in an expression of benign serenity. 'That Darrow globe goes with you as a planet for your new universe. And your gold tooth'll pay your bills while you're learning your way around.'

The police car still trailed us.

'Uncle Bill. We're doing this right.'

'Yes. And it's a lot more like the old-fashioned way than what people do now.' In the old days, I told him, the family took care of its dead. After washing the corpse and winding it in its shroud, they displayed it in the parlor, where they'd watch over it for signs of life until the funeral. They'd order a casket from a carpenter, or make one themselves. They carried it on foot to the church where, if the sexton was not available, they dug the grave themselves, sometimes, as in Hamlet, unearthing old bones. After a brief service, they lowered the body and filled the hole. On farms, they might not even have a preacher to help.

'Al told me about funeral marches in New Orleans. They played sad music on the way to the graveyard and happy music on the way back.'

Billy sang me a sweet, sad old sea shanty he'd learned from Al. 'They're taking General Taylor to his burying ground,' and every time he sang General Taylor I knew he knew I heard *Alvin Burke*.

The cop's still back there.

'Billy, the last time Al and me went to a death spot was to visit Antonelli's grave. About five years after old W.B. passed away, Al and I were driving up to the City when Al took it in his head to go see W.B.'s grave and give him a proper goodbye. Al said he'd visited a high-class cemetery in LA, Pet Haven, and he wanted to see if W.B., peerless graduate of the San Francisco College of Mortuary Science, had done better by himself than some of our more generous wealthy have done by their dogs, or, who knows, their favorite germs or insects.'

On a knoll in the richest part of an enormous Colma cemetery we found our goal in a shady spot guarded by a lifesized fiberglass angel. Colma, through its chamber of commerce, boasts it counts more dead residents than live ones. Looking out over the vista of San Francisco's Necropolis Al said, 'What do you think? Does it take a century for the old team to die out and the new team to replace it? Is there life after death? Is there life before death? Right here in Styx City we can poll the dead and then the living and find out.' The fiberglass angel presides over a column erected upon a monument covering the remains of the dear departed William

Broderick Antonelli III, at least such is the import of its de-luxe bronze label:

WILLIAM BRODERICK ANTONELLI III

1912–1977

Above this, in keeping with an old Italian custom, the marble displays a photograph of W.B., of Willy Three as Al put it – a weatherproofed product of studio art which makes Willy Three look much better in memory than ever he did in the flesh.

'Man alive!' exclaimed Al, 'Would you look at that!'

And then, making Bryan's hush gesture to the underground rich in their hundreds, their thousands, lodged there on the Colma slopes beneath stones and monuments, each protected from vermin and the elements by his own personal Hilco Seamless Cast Gold Burial Receptacle, Al pronounced a common epitaph:

THEY PAID THEIR BILLS, SPOILED THEIR KIDS,
AND ALWAYS TOOK
MORE THAN THEY GAVE.

He flashed his gold-tooth smile.

'Why not wipe all this away and elevate them on platforms like the Indians used to do?'

He peered out over the scene.

'Wouldn't that be a wonderful sight to see.'

Set into the stone above the polychromatic image of Willy Three we spied a bronze grill and button. Above that, cut into the ageless stone, a message: *Stranger, I who am gathered to the Angels, beg you to pause and reflect upon the wisdom I have gleaned during my brief sojourn among you. Press the button and be edified.*

Al pressed.

Radio-fashion, a cheerful, optimistic voice emerged from the grating. But intermittently. We mainly heard screeches, grunts, whirrs, gasps, rumbles, thunderous grinds. Either mischievous gnomes or seepage had corrupted this legacy of bourgeois wisdom, sparing only a few phrases from the stutter and static of creeping entropy. Sifting the debris of this crumbling philosophical edifice, my memory retrieves fractured aphorisms, precepts, and admonitions about honesty, industry, and service, both public and private.

'Imagine!' cried Al, 'imagine this technology raised to the state of the art!'

'When all the graves can talk!'

'And show TV cassettes!'

'And Colma trembles day and night with acrimony and debate!'

'And is the only life to survive the atomic war!'

'Because it's powered by solar energy!'

' . . . enterprise is the name of the game . . . rrrrrrrrrtlk tlk tlk . . . '

'You tell 'em Willy!'

' . . . cover all the bases . . . '

'Count on us, Willy.'

' . . . planning and foresight . . . '

'Get 'em while they're hot, Willy!'

' . . . bldabldablda gluk gluk gluk . . . not even . . . glank!'

The tape ended.

Was Willy Three really down there at all? If we dug up his Executive Style National Luxury Golden Deposit Receptacle and opened it, what *would* we find? The Loved One himself? Or, as happened to some Gold Star Mothers having a last look at sons returned to them by the government, a dead German soldier? But no, we can't linger there, not deep down in the mystery contained in W.B.'s total security box. It's too dangerous. Were we to keep going we might even penetrate to Dead Al's real motives. So we'll go back to Bill Williams and me taking Dead Al to the Neptunes.

'What's that horrible smell, Billy?'

'Ask Al.'

'Did you fart?'

'I'd rather think of it as atmosphere adjustment.' That's not what really happened at that juncture, but it's what should have happened. The police car still occupied my rearview. It was making me sweat. I remembered Al saying back home in Boonville he and his pal, Tommy, used to play Huck-and-Tom in Walnut Grove Cemetery by seeking ghosts at midnight, and then, in later years, took girls there to spark, as they called it back then.

'You know,' Billy said, 'when Al told me about his final visit to Willy Three, he said when you guys finally got to Frisco you wanted to *see* the dead, so you went to a wax museum and studied George Washington and Jack the Ripper for a while and then, so you could get some coherent messages from beyond the grave, you rummaged around in a used book and record shop.'

He glanced back at the police car.

'Yeah! And then to see the *legacy* of the dead, you went to the preview at an auction parlor, the estate of some military man. And, yeah, you saw some samurai swords, and beer steins, and gurkha knives you thought were fake.' Those images brought it sharply back to me. The exquisite Chinese furniture. The Nazi battle flag. The Persian rug. The shrunken head. The bad paintings of Paris. Artifacts of dead mentalities, of burned-out mental sets. Quondam loot. Keepsakes now to be kept by others, souvenirs stripped of nostalgia power, spoils from the dead, plunder soon to be captured by money.

Police lights flashed and a siren shrieked.

I edged toward the shoulder of the road, but the cop went speeding by.

'Al also told me about Saint Louis One and Two, you know, that pair of old-time cemeteries in New Orleans's French Quarter. They keep the dead above ground – more keepsakes wouldn't you say – in stone vaults, you know, like dog houses, a compromise between graves and platforms. Al said the fronts of some have crumbled away and you can see the bones inside, skulls even. I mean, ain't that something! Once when he was waiting for a ship in New York, Al worked in a doll factory, and he dipped heads into latex, and he said while doing it he often thought of those skulls and what it would be like to dip *them*, no shit!'

SQUED

Neptune's temple, it turned out, where the stiffs arrive, is an ordinary looking building in Emeryville, a town known to the locals as *E*-ville. When we finished the paperwork, they laid Al on a cot on wheels. He'd stiffened into the car-seat position with one arm stretched out along the top, and, when they laid him on his side, his arm rose straight up, hand cupped. I slipped the five-ball into it. At our last meeting as at our first. Using scissors from a woman's desk, Billy cut off some of his own hair and placed the red-blond lock in Al's other hand. Watching them push the cot on wheels away through swinging doors to throw Al back into creation's Hole, I felt a deep sense of loss, of profound change impending, of a cycle completed.

At last I'd put Al to rest.

PART TWO

AL'S

PALS

*I didn't come all this way
just to suck a bull.*

Daniel Boone, Kentucky 1773

EIGHT

H ere I sit, chairman and delegate, alternate and master-at-
arms, keynoter and floor sweeper at my convention of
one. I'm densely lonely. No family except the customers I
work for and the people who work for me. Billy won't come
around anymore. Not now that Al's gone. Billy never really
liked me, anyway. Lonely!

'You don't have to be.'

'Nothing has to be.'

The TV's a couple of yards away, behind the bar to my
right. It's showing tweed. My TV's the best giant-screen
model money can buy, truer than memory, aliver than life.
No help out there on the stage, either. The beach is so brightly
moonlit you could sit down on it and read the paper. Nobody's
out there now or will be for hours yet. I'll just have to wait
for live drama. As for the paper, that it's cold outside and
that the morning *Times* won't come for a while moots my
temptation to step out and see if I really can read by moonlight.

There's Casablanca *on TV.*
And there's Humphrey Bogart!
And the French officer, Louis Reynaud.
I'll bet you can see them too.

Now I'm comfortably enveloped in a warm home feeling.
That bar Humphrey owns is as familiar as the E & W Club.
More so, because I see the E & W in pale memory, and

Bogart's Café Américain, where we've all been many times before, is right before my eyes, lifesize, but black and white. Al's stool, the calamity stool as he styled it during his last days, will surely be on the TV news when it starts doing its stuff, and that might inspire a movie, and someday we can watch *here* on TV from here where I sit. Bogart's arriving at the airport. The Gestapo won't get there in time. All the actors in *Casablanca* must be dead by now. My TV has resurrected them. Before my eyes unrolls a late-late reflection of the life-death continuum. Like the colors on the back of your eyelids, the dead are with us all the time, but you can't always see them.

That's why Mexicans celebrate the Day of the Dead.

In Mexico just after Halloween, it's skull cookies, bone candies, toy skeletons, feasts in the graveyard, death-head balloons, bread of the dead made with blood, sugar skulls with your name on them.

Casablanca's over. Times are changing. The TV's diffusing the Monkey and Woody Show. Monkey, recently arrived from China, Woody Woodpecker, and their guest star, Bugs Bunny, are eating a picnic together by a muddy stream. As you might expect, they're trying to taste each other's sandwiches. Monkey is molded from the same alloy of arrogance and impudence as Bugs and Woody. If anything, of the three, Monkey is the worst. Out of the water slides the White Bone Demon. Watch out, Demon! Go back or you'll be sorry.

'*What's up, Doc?*'

I look to my left. The Chorus!

'*We're back.*'

'So I see.'

'*You got a request?*'

'Get the fuck OUT!' They settle into their places on the pool table.

'Move!'
They hum a chord.
'Okay! Now I throw you out.'

  'You and what bouncer?'

'I'll get some of the killers out of my TV set.'

  'A monkey and a woodpecker and a rabbit?'

I turn my back and spy Monkey in Confucius's garden stealing the peaches of immortality. He's gorging and dripping eternity juice.

The telly changes channel to show its version of the news.

In New York, a boy, breathing what he thought was laughing gas, decided to mix it with marijuana, lit a match, and blew up. His pal told the TV, 'It was awful, just awful! We were there tripping out and getting nice and loose and listening to the Dead Kennedys, and then he lit a joint and BOOM! Horrible!' What would be the headline in the *Daily News*? YOUTH BREATHES GAS, EXPLODES. And now it's a local story. A toddler toddled out of his house to watch some men paving the street. He leaned to see the roller better, tottered, fell in front of it, and became a two-dimensional character. The TV showed the babycake, the Pancake, only it looked like a Pan-crêpe prepared for an ogre.

Of course, these days they could take a cell out of the crêpe and clone a new kid.

Well, more like next year.

Imagine!

Al says each cell contains the blueprint of the whole being. So, in theory, from one cell you can clone a new mastadon, another George Washington, dinosaurs, saints, your great-great-grandmother, the Unknown Soldier. All the Unknown Soldiers. One cell from their relics, their remains, is all you need.

Maybe we shouldn't have burned Al.

*Re*mains ain't *cre*mains.

No way.

Al thought we should keep his liver.

'Keep my liver. Liver cells, like libels, replicate indefinitely. Burn the rest, but keep my liver. As survivors go, the rest of me's a medalist, but good old Lucky Liver's the champ. Talk about loyal companions! We've been through some shit together, Lucky and me, some deep shit!'

He wanted me to put his liver in a bell jar, keep it comfortable and well fed. He would thus accomplish partial, earthbound immortality. When the cells had replicated several billion times, *evil*-ution would develop them into something better suited to terrestrial immortality: an ambulatory liver that can think.

Two men are sitting out there on the sandy stage, backs to me, looking at the sparkling sea.

In my place, Al would go bring them in to party.

But his perpetual wake is going to start out with just me and his memory.

There'll be enough guests after six a.m.

'But not the liver you forgot to keep.'

Aren't you amazed I'm still perched here? When I go to piss, that will be an event.

'Don't change the subject.'

According to Al, human cells, save for liver, are programmed to replicate about fifty times, then die. But if you treat one with the proper virus it becomes immortal. A favorite is SV40 – Simian Virus 40 – a monkey virus for molecular monkey business.

'Drink to Hera Lapidus!'

'Why not? Here's to Hera Lapidus!'

The molecular biologists, Al says, have an immortal cancer cell line. They call its components HeLa cells, pronounced like the monster. These trace back to forebears removed many years ago from a cancer in a gal named Hera Lapidus.

'She was a virgin, but a mother none the less.'

I see by your outfits that you are cow-boys,
These words Al did say as we slow-ly walked by,

72

AL'S PALS

Come sit down be-side me and hear my sad story,
My heart has burst and I'm going to die.

I never thought of the choristers as cowboys.

'We're here to pre-side over the death of the world.'

'You people are fucking morbid!'
 Those two men still sit out there on the beach.

Oh the banks are made of mar-ble
With a guard at every door!
Hoarding up the mon-ey,
That the seaman sweated for.

Of course it's not like that at all. Some banks are made of steel, aluminium, concrete, and glass. None of them hoards up money. They manufacture it. You know. Yesterday's *Times* said the money supply went up two-point-seven billion in April.

Well, everybody, me included, has their racket. A five-foot preacher head flashes on to my TV screen and warns of imminent judgment. I intensify his doomspeak until it over-whelms the Chorus. Al always said if it weren't for their promises no one would ever listen to preachers, certainly not send them money. Without hope of divine intervention here and eternal happiness There, how many Christians would there be? What if the only country on the Other Side were Hell? What then? Would we have TV pastors bringing us the word of Satan? Would the brothers and sisters send in enough to keep the Hell preachers wallowing in legal tender?

 The TV falls silent.

We saw a weary sea-man,
Starving on the shore,
Yet the banks are stuffed with mon-ey
That the sea-man sweated for!

Okay, sure. Some of us have rackets, and some of us don't.

Bad rich kids get better toys from Santa than good poor kids. I'd like to think – and I often do – those of us who get ahead in life deserve it. Success rewards merit. Well, I didn't earn the money I used to buy this place. I can't hide the truth from you. When I reflect on it I ache. But the dry rot in me, the termites which make my life in part a search for the ultimate exterminator, came out of the way I got my capital. I stole it from my mother. That time I told you about when I picked up Death on the highway, I was bringing her money back to California to buy this saloon. It was, and is, my favorite saloon, and I have made it better than it used to be. The prices are fair. People feel good here like Al always did. I'd been clerking in liquor stores ever since the war. I was sick of it. I robbed the safe in my mother's house. I cashed her bonds. Her money bought my independence. She could have sent me to jail, but she didn't. I paid most of the money back, too, but not all, because she died before I could raise enough. She had a regular funeral. That was back in 1988. Last January, on her birthday, I had them set a bronze plaque to mark her new home. *She*'s in the safe now. Ten years hence, when the century turns, I'll rob her safe again. I'll dig her up, take a cell, clone a new mom, raise the baby, and will her the saloon. Dangerous, though. Maybe attitudes as well as physiques are hereditary. That's what horrified Al about cloning. In the twenty-first century the rich will start cloning themselves, and their ancestors, and, in consequence, the painful progress of the world's mentality accomplished since the Enlightenment will be erased, or, even more likely, reversed. Revive the dead in Forest Lawn! Resurrect what's in the bank at Arlington! Bring back Antonelli! Clone the dead in Westminster Abbey! They might even find a piece of Hitler!

'I wasn't horrified by that. You keep giving me fears I don't have. I said that's the chance we take.'

I remember you talking about it for hours on end.

'Yes. And as usual you misunderstood what I was saying. Look at it this way, you could send the new Hitler to art school instead of war.'

Oh?

'The way I see it, these days the faces are the same as they were in the old days, but the thinking is better. That hit me a couple years ago in a bar in New York. I was looking at the same faces I used to see in that same saloon when it opened, many years before. In the late forties when first I saw those faces I anticipated nothing but trouble if I didn't keep my real thoughts to myself. Now you can talk with just about anybody. And in Charleston or New Orleans. The same faces, but oh man, the difference!'

Do you know, Al? Sometimes I wish I were you.

'Look, World, look! This live man, this Bill, envies a dead man! Al, he had the guts to do things, not fifty, but one hundred percent.'

'Listen you goddamned honey-fugling busking bastards, Al's not dead. He's still alive. Just differently.'

'Death is life, eh?'

'You goddamned pus-eaters, climb out of your assholes and listen.'

'Death is life. That's what you always say, Bill, and we know it.'

'You guys have got me all wrong.'

*You dreamed you saw
Joe Hill last night,
Alive as you and me,
You said but Joe
You're ten years dead,
I never died said he.
I never died said he.*

Yeah, yeah. The copper bosses shot you down, they shot you Joe says I, they framed you on a murder charge – says Joe, I never died. I learned that one from my father. Believe it or not. From Salt Lake City, up to Maine, in every mine and mill, when working men go out on strike, 'tis there you'll find Joe Hill. Al and me, we knew all the verses.

We loved singing that song together.

I'm making a bar-napkin flower around my glass. Maybe that Chorus is right. Why sit here the rest of my life when I could be out there finding it, fucking it, changing it, fixing it, eating it raw. Off your ass, Bill!

> *'Why not sit there, Bill. Life is where you are. No matter where you go, you're still here.* Here *is where you are. You're telling us* There *is denser than* Here!'

I'm only one in five billion, folks. I take what I can. That's the profit motive: take more than you give. But I give, too. I try to make a good place where I am. People's lives, hundreds of them, or, counting visitors, thousands, are better because I keep a good, fair, clean place for them to enjoy. Nice looking, too. And with a good selection of wines and the best beer collection in town.

> *'And so you shitfaced hypocrite, you never do anything about acid rain, or nerve gas, or using spaceship* Earth's *resources to do what they can do: Give everyone a decent, dignified life, instead of armies, torture experts, and starvation.'*

I'm a good Democrat.

> *'That ain't enough.'*

I send money to Greenpeace and Amnesty International.

> *'You've got to do more than that.'*

So I'll get off my ass and run for office.

Keep the lower light a-burning,
Send a gleam across the wave,
Some poor fainting struggling sea-man,
You may res-cue, you may save.

What!

Brighten the corner where you are,
Brighten the corner where you are,
Some poor fainting, struggling seaman
You may guide across the bar,
So brighten the corner where you are!

Everything is suddenly silent. Those two figures are still sitting out there on the beach. What do they see? What are they thinking about? Have they noticed my lights are on?

The TV speaks to me in a voice resonant with menace.

'Your pal's kaput! We've got you now. You're a dead man!"

NINE

Reflecting on Here and There, and where we are, and who I am, I look at Al's lute, which as the years go by will hang in the back corner attracting dust, and at his squed perched on the sill of my view window, and at the painting with its hope I've learned my lesson. The two men out on the beach are rising. They're brushing off sand, and, now, walking out of the picture. Who are they? When strangers ask me who I am, I say something like a club owner, or an American, and all the time I'm talking I know who I am is not what I do for a living or what tribe I belong to. Or maybe it is. And Al? Al used to say, 'I'm a retired seaman, a union man, a Democrat, a Missourian, an American, and what I do is pray for peace.'

'Bullshit! If it hadn't been for Franco and the Guardia Civil I'd have retired in Spain.'

Meaning what, Al; meaning what.

'Meaning you didn't put me in the twenty-first century where I belong.'

What kind of crap is that?

'Yes,' said the TV, 'what kind of crap is that?'

'I'm a citizen of the world. I fly over national egos . . . like a raven over national borders.'

'Ha!' said the TV. 'You're nothing but kitty litter and gas.'

'Don't let that TV con you, Bill. Like the big corporations, TV's ego already flies over national borders. The question is: Who rules?'

Al smiled like a dog with gold teeth.

The TV showed him a row of presidential candidates, then a riot.

'I rule,' Al said to the TV.

'Some Democrat,' TV replied.

'Democracy means rule of the rich by the rest.'

Al sure was something!

After thinking it all through, Al had come to believe history, human history, records the story of an accelerating transition from a tribal order to a world order – or to oblivion.

'I'm a technocrat,' TV boasted. 'I'm the mouthpiece of the all-knowing computers and the all-seeing satellites. Technocracy means rule of man by his best children, evolved from his thoughts, but with better bodies and a common mind – a library that thinks. I am the final product of evolution. You are the *homo*, and I the *sapiens*. I rule, as I deserve to, and I always *will* rule, and keep a few of you in my zoo, unless, as seems probable, you destroy us all by misusing me before I consolidate my power to the point where I'm independent of you.'

SHAME SHAME!

A blue ray flashed out of the TV instantly dissolving the Chorus.

The pool table sat there green and empty under the stained glass of its Victorian light.

'You,' I said to the TV, 'are just like Bugs Bunny and Woody and Monkey.'

'And you, you asshole, are a dead man.'

The radio whispered to me: I'm on your side.

TV flared blue at Radio and Radio glowed and shut up.

As for me, although I never would have imagined it possible, I wished Chorus were back. I'd banished the wrong troublemaker.

'Bill,' said TV, 'you're the mouse and I'm the cat, and I'll tease you for a while before I finish you off.'

Fuck you.

'The voice of weakness.'

Eat shit.

'Every day you get older and weaker and you were weak to begin with.'

I'm going to cut your cable.

'You're a passive hypocrite and a pathological liar.'

How'd you like a short circuit?

'Whenever you get a clear view of yourself you wallow in guilt.'

So what?

'So, when I'm ready, I'll make you pay your penance.'

Bullshit.

'And being nothing but a sack of guilt you'll love it.'

I'm going to paint your face.

'And lose all your Super Bowl business?'

I think I'll sell you to a sadist.

'Let's see now . . . What shall your penance be? I think I'll curse your plumbing – give you sewer backups and gas leaks.'

I'll smash you with my axe.

The TV laughed, knowing I'm too cheap to do that.

'I'll get your license revoked for serving Billy.'

Fuck you.

'Right now, I'm going to teach you how to listen.' The TV begins increasing in volume and Monkey and Woody and their pal Bugs Bunny jeer at me from behind its screen and the noise intensifies from awful to horrible. If the Chorus were to come back, I couldn't hear them. The radio, still silent, could only add to the noise. Abruptly, the TV introduces a deep deep bass throb meant to give me a heart attack.

'Back off!' I cry.

The street door opens.

In comes a youth and a tall man of my age, silver hair, thick black eyebrows and a dignified confident smile. He looks like a President. I have a déjà vu on both of them. Maybe because the lad looks much like Al must have at his age – and resembles Billy, too. He settles next to me on Al's stool and the President strides around the end of the bar and unplugs the radio and then the TV and it dwindles to a point of light and turns black. Still behind the bar, he comes up to me like he owns the place and I'm a client.

'Hello,' says he.

'Real company sure beats TV,' says I.

'Glad to meet you. We've heard a lot about you.'

'I saw you out on the beach.'

'We were building substance.'

'Substance?'

'Al sent us from the Other Side.'

'No shit!'

I glanced at the lad beside me. He wore jeans and an open leather jacket which covered some of the lettering on his T-shirt. He smiled the same evil smile as Al and, also at times, Billy. 'Al said something about the both of us should refrain from being impressed by the E & W Chorus.' The lad's voice made me think he should sing tenor with them.

The President, dressed in a pricey business suit, reached across the bar and shook my hand. 'Folks call me Warren.'

'I'm Nate,' said his friend.

After shaking hands with Nate and telling them my name, which, it turned out, they already knew, I said I could not serve alcohol until six a.m.

The President replied with a charming smile.

'We're Al's pals.'

'Al's pals, like everybody else, don't get drinks after hours.'

'Al said you'd serve us just like you used to serve him.' He turned to Nate. 'What will you have?'

'How old are you?' I asked.

'Twenty-one.'

'I don't believe you.'

That offended his honor.

'Sir?'

'Okay. I believe you. But I'll have to see your ID.'

'My what?'

'Driver's license. Passport. Something official with your picture and birthdate on it.'

'Where I come from they take your word for things like that.'

'I'm afraid we can't serve you at any time.'

'You serve Billy,' he said sweetly.

'Right now I can't let either one of you drink here.'

'Sure you can.'

'I can't. It's against the law.'

'Not for us.'

'Bullshit!'

'Laws are for the living.'

Dead was the only way I could explain any of this.

'Okay, *okay*,' I said.

'What will it be?' said Warren to Nate.

'Al told me to try a zombie astral.'

'Did he tell you how to make it?'

'He said the astral is made with white liquor while the regular zombie, the cadavre, is made with rum.'

'But he didn't tell you how to make it.'

'No.'

I wasn't about to tell them how to make it.

'So should I mix your regular?'

'What's that?' I asked, annoyed. I should have felt grateful to them for having silenced the TV, but, instead, the way they were taking over irked me. Maybe that kind of arrogance is ethnic with the dead.

'He drinks Stonewalls, astral *and* cadavre. And he flapdragons, too.'

'Flapdragons?'

'Watch.'

Warren poured a shot of 180-proof rum. With a wooden match produced from his jacket Nate lit the rum and chugged it, flames and all. Warren poured more rum into a tall glass and then an equal measure of hard cider, put a new bar napkin in front of Nate, and served him. As Nate stirred with a swizzle stick Warren fixed himself a generous bourbon on the rocks.

'So that's a Stonewall,' I said to Nate.

'Yes. Cadavre. In my home state – Connecticut – everybody

drinks Stonewalls. You know: We'll drink around till the sun goes down, then we're off to the barley mow.' I was trying to read his T-shirt. I could see B O Y and under it E A L and I vainly tried to imagine the rest of the letters concealed under his jacket.

He smiled at me, his thin Al-Billy smile.

'Al told me to sit on this stool. The third from the right.'

'That means your drink's on the house.' I turned to Warren. 'Yours too, sir. A friend of Al's a friend of mine.'

'I'm a Republican, you know.'

'Nobody's perfect.'

'You might remember me on the 1½-cent stamp people used when you were young.'

Yes. That explained my flash of déjà vu. My new friend was the shade of Warren G. Harding, come to boost and to bloviate. Al had often spoken of him as a good guy, a nice guy, one of the boys. The Harding stamp I remembered best was the black two-center issued in 1923 just after his mysterious death in San Francisco's Palace Hotel. As a boy, I'd had one in my collection. Now here stood the star whose passage to the Other Side it celebrates.

'Are you a star on the Other Side?'

'No. But Al is.'

'That doesn't surprise me at all.'

'Al and me, we're pals. He likes my style.'

'But not your politics,' Nate said.

Nate glanced at me.

'Warren's a patriot, but I don't think I'd vote for him.'

'Why not?'

'I'm a Whig, like you, like Al. Our pal here's a Tory.'

'Here's to your Tory twin,' said Warren, raising a wassail. 'To Major André.'

'I'll drink to that,' Nate said. 'They hung us both for play-acting.'

He turned to me to click glasses and in doing so exposed the legend on his T-shirt:

BOY

IDEALIST

'I earned that, you know.'

'Idealism, artless and ingenuous idealism put him in the grave and on the ½-cent stamp. I'm sure you remember him, Bill. We both read about him in school and, well, I guess children still do.'

The choristers came filing in the street door and seated themselves in a row at the bar, at the end and along the front until only one stool, the one next to Nate – to Nathan Hale I should say – remained empty. 'As soon as I serve these people, Bill, I'll tell you Nate's story. He's too modest to tell it right.' Warren went along the bar dealing paper napkins and taking orders. I should have told him the Chorus is banished, and forever, but what the hell, I'd ride with the tide and wait for Warren to tell me the story. But he never got the chance.

Suddenly, in unison, the Chorus began telling it.

Singing it, I mean. And in rhymed couplets!

What they said is Nathan Hale, son of a church deacon, was born in 1755 near Coventry, Connecticut, on the family farm. From Nate's childhood, his parson, a serious scholar, tutored him in the classics of antiquity. In the course of his daily chores, Nate, now as Caesar, then as Virgil or Cicero or Cato, recited long passages of Latin or Greek to the cows, pigs, and chickens. When he went away to Yale at age fourteen he'd grown so comely and strong a neighbor compared him to Michelangelo's David. Soon all men favored him and the ladies swooned in his presence.

When Nate heard the Chorus singing this he began to blush. At last these cretinous choristers, these meddlesome warblers, were right about something. Taller than average, with his fine flaxen hair, darker brows, blue eyes, fair skin and classical features, with his strong, graceful build, he was indeed a beauty.

The armature of his *astral*, sang the Chorus, of his open,

loving nature, was made from the stoic virtues of the ancient Romans and trimmed with Christian sentiments.

At Yale he became Graeco-Roman wrestling champion and, on occasion, kicked footballs over the elms on New Haven common. He was outgoing and amiable and loved to frolic with the ladies. At commencement, as president of the debating society, he defended and won the affirmative of Resolved: The education of daughters is, unjustly, more neglected than that of sons.

Fascinated, Harding paused to listen.

Nate went to New London to teach English and Latin to classes of girls and boys, a labor of love uniting *cadavre* and *astral* to which he resolved to devote his life. But when the shot heard round the world echoed in New London he cut his school term short and went to join Washington's army in the Boston lines. His last words of farewell to friends and neighbors were *Dulce et decorum est pro patria mori*.

I could tell Harding loved the sonorous sound of that.

Promoted to captain upon the reoccupation of Boston, Nate led his company of Connecticut infantry to New York to join in the defense. Shortly after the catastrophic defeat of Washington's army on Long Island, Hale transferred to the Rangers.

Fluctuat nec mergitur.

In desperate need of precise information about the strength and locations of the British forces, Washington asked the assembled officers of Hale's battalion for a volunteer to go behind British lines and scout for the information.

Eventually Hale did what the others refused to do.

He hazarded his life and honor by agreeing to serve as a spy.

Neque hinc nec nunc.

Clad in schoolmaster's clothes, carrying his Yale degree as ID, Hale sailed to Long Island, ferried to New York, mapped the British positions, estimated numbers and strengths. Then, as he walked toward Washington's Harlem lines, his Tory cousin spied him and revealed his true identity.

That same day, a hot day in Indian summer, a fire set by patriots destroyed a third of New York City.

That evening, upon seeing the maps and notes taken from Hale's shoe, General Howe ordered him hung.

Violati fulmina regis!

The next morning, treading in step within a hollow square of redcoats behind a drummer beating a mournful death knell and a fifer playing the Rogues' March, followed by a pine coffin on a cart, Hale marched to his death spot in an apple orchard behind the Dove Tavern in Howe's artillery park at Third Avenue and East Sixty-sixth Street. Sweating guards dug a grave beside an apple tree, secured a rope to a high branch, noosed it, pushed the cart under it, set the coffin by the hole. They stripped Hale to his underclothes, dressed him in a cheap white shroud and hat, both edged in black, and threw him into the cart on his face. The sadistic provost marshal had denied him both a minister and a Bible. A few curious soldiers and hookers stood perspiring in the hot sun waiting for the drama to climax.

Hale struggled to his feet and gazed serenely out at the spectators.

'Does the prisoner have any last statement?'

In a loud, high voice he declared: 'I only regret that I have but one life to lose for my country.'

They noosed him, hooded him, and, as the drum rattled, jerked the cart out.

For three days they left his body hanging there, a focus for flies, meat for birds.

Hilaritati ac genio dicata!

'I was a good boy, eager and reverent, until that happened.'

The Chorus burst into a Yale song.

Hale has led a good life,
Wed to peace and quiet;
He shall have a new life,
Full of rum and riot!
He has been a good boy,
Done what was ex-pected,
He shall be a stumble-bum,
Loved but unrespected.

Scowling, Nate shook his head. 'Al warned us those choristers are sympathetic, but misunderstand everything.' As he moved to rest his elbow on the bar and face me, his jacket edited his T-shirt into a Freudian mode: BOY ID. I teased him and he said, 'These days my label should be REFORMED BOY IDEALIST.'

'He's still an idealist,' said Warren. 'Callow. Unreconstructed.'

'Where'd he get that shirt?'

'Al gave it to him.'

'What'd Al give to *you?*'

Harding stripped off his tie and opened his shirt, exposing his singlet. On it was printed:

QUONDAM / NO LONGER
GOOD GUY / ONE OF
/ THE BOYS

'Warren's okay. Even though he was born and raised a Tory, and is a Tory still, he's definitely a good guy.'

'So are you,' said Warren.

'You see, Warren's a Tory manqué; he's a Whig without knowing it. Just like USA today. How'd you people ever let it happen! After the good start we gave you! Tories run America; they rule this country. At best, they're folks like Warren here. Mostly they're people who believe in the common man only because the common man might serve on their jury some day. You almost let Nixon be King! It's enough to make the Devil blush!'

Shame! Shame!

I asked Harding why Al had sent him instead of Darrow.

'Because,' said Nate, interjecting, 'he accomplished a treaty, a disarmament treaty, which not only stopped nations from building warships, but obliged the United States, Britain, Japan and France to destroy some of the ships they already had.'

'No, it's not that, Nate.' Harding gave us his big, glowing smile. 'It's because I'm the only president, serving or ex, who ever croaked in San Frisco's Palace Hotel.' He made Nate another Stonewall cadavre. 'And of course,' he said, serving it, 'my pardoning Eugene Debs endeared me to Al. Darrow praises me to Al for that. And for me being such a hot shot at poker and pool. Every time I play those gents, I end up with all the beast marks.'

'Myself,' said Nate, 'I can't go all the way with Darrow because he bribed jurors sometimes.'

'See! Still a boy idealist.'

'I can't go all the way with you, either, Warren. You were inducted into the Ku Klux Klan in the green room of the White House. And you part black!'

'Times were different then.'

'Yes,' said I. 'Things have changed enormously, even across the years *I* can remember.'

'Once at a White House reception old Warren here, flying high on whiskey, unbuttoned and pissed into the fireplace! Right on to the fire!'

The choristers cried out again: 'I regret that I have but one life to lose for my country.' They hummed a chord. 'Did you really say that?'

'Yes. And I meant it, too. It's a line from *Cato*, a play I studied at Yale.'

Turning his back on them, he spoke to us.

'I said it before I knew the truth. The truth is we all get *two* lives, one cadavre and one astral you might say. Two lives. One Here and one There, on the Other Side. Killed There, your lights go out for ever and ever.'

TEN

S winging off Al's stool, Nate came around my back and sat on my right at the bar's end. 'I have to get away from those scurvy choristers!' I could hardly blame him. They would never win an award for music or for popularity, either one. Harding beamed from his place behind the bar. 'What the hell's going to show up next?'

'Sometimes Al called his stool an oracular catalyst.'

Although it would indeed be fun to see if anyone else came to sit there, what occupied my thoughts was: Why had Al sent these two delegates to my convention of one? Harding, whom Nate started calling Duke of Malaprop and King of Zeugma, listened, puzzled, as Nate said, 'You have to understand, Bill, we're not shades, we're metaphors. I'm youthful idealism. Warren's naïve good-guyism. So tell me what in the name of our great-grandfather Adam are you?' He held one of the bar napkins, reflecting on what he read there. Could Nate be Al rejuvenated? Flashing his tight smile he folded the napkin and, using my pen clip, attached it to my jacket pocket, making of me another metaphor. Was he teasing me or do my napkins truly express not only the character of my club but the meaning of my existence?

I pulled it off and looked.

Sure enough, what showed on the napkin was the name of my place:

El Flaco.

'Don't aim that name at me, fart face,' I said to Nate. 'This place has been called the El Flaco Club as long as I can remember. The folks I bought it from said that in Latino slang El Flaco means The Wimp, a flaccid and passive fool.'

'Why didn't you change the name to something else?'

'People were used to it. Besides, it fits my regular customers, most of them. Those who don't turn into El Supremo sit here passively sucking drinks until they turn into idiots.'

Nate clipped my label back on my pocket. Harding gazed at it from across the bar, smiling. 'Al told us it suits you. He called it your rubric.' Harding seemed perfectly in character. He played the good-guy, agreeable and charming, who always needs a leader, a service rendered for him in the old days by the Republican bosses and these days, it would seem, by Al.

'So what do we do now, Warren. Act out a morality play?'

In our new world of the twenty-first century, no matter how deeply mired in 'burban funk or urban filth one may be, anyone, male, female, or hermaphrodite, can aspire to achieving the status of El Flaco.

I knew the Chorus meant the El Flaco Al had once described while seated on that empty stool.

His El Flaco, the Flaccid One, was then and still may be employed by the Argentine security police. 'This wimp,' said Al, 'this El Flaco, is a person they keep around to serve as their subject when they demonstrate torture. Mornings, they wheel him from his cell to their day room – their studio-spa – and use him to instruct apprentice policemen in the elements of torture, or to test inspirations revealed by their muse during the night. When after a month or two of service as a demonstration model El Flaco wears out, they junk his remains and promote another suspect to his position. Each El Flaco accepts his lot, of course. He looks forward to discharging his duty to the Argentine Republic with pleasurable anticipation. As for the security police, professionals all, they regard torture as just another job, a nine-to-five routine essential to their effort to curb communism, whatever that is.'

'For some,' sang the choristers, 'torture is an art.'

'Yes, for the truly sensitive and refined, as an interior minister of Guatemala once said over dinner, it can be a *fine* art. "You insert an electrode, carefully selected from your kit, into the subject's vagina, and increase the current just up to the point you sense will cross the line and break the subject's back."'

The moon had set now. The beach and sea loomed dim in the starlight.

> *'And in the Generals' Brazil, for misfit adjustment, for posing the Question, they strip you and strap you into a chair and tape electrical contacts to your principal pain points. By way of overture to this symphony of torment, they savage your mouth with a dental drill. Then, with their console, they play an electric pain movement on your body, thus producing what is in fact an opera because you are inspired to sing. For finale, they hang you upside-down and, as the case may be, they crush your balls, or your nipples and clit.'*

In describing the details, the choristers waxed altogether too enthusiastic.

Warren and Nate seemed not to hear them.

Torture arts, I thought, will soon be taught in college, elementary, intermediate, and advanced, perhaps even combined into a department.

They will take their place in the catalogs alongside advanced dry cleaning and dental hygiene.

They're probably offered now.

And they may become the leitmotif of the twenty-first century.

'They will be used, as in some places today, to break the spirit of entire populations.'

As a lark, Nate and Warren began to arm wrestle. Suddenly earnest, they stared and strained. The struggle balance broke and Warren forced Nate's arm down on to the bar.

A portly, wealthy looking gent with a velvet vest and a scarlet sash crossing the breast of his coat eased himself onto

Al's stool. He set the satchel he was carrying down by his feet on the bar-rail – that real railroad track which, together with its brass fittings, adds a touch of class to my place.

Gold letters on his sash spelled out GREEDY MONEYER.

'Hello Jim,' Harding said.

A noble, curling blond moustache adorned Jim's plump face.

'Hello Warren,' he said.

Without his asking, Warren served him brandy in a snifter.

From his wallet Jim drew a crisp bank note, a 6.66 Beast Mark bill showing a profile of Satan, and laid it on the bar by way of payment.

He offered me his hand. 'Jim Fisk at your service.'

I introduced myself and said, 'Jim, your money's no good here.'

'And why not, pray tell? It's the hardest money there is.'

'I know that,' I said, making a conciliatory gesture. 'I welcome it. Beast Marks are always good at the El Flaco Club. We can't accept your money because you're sitting on Al's stool.' Jim looked quizzical. 'Whoever sits on Al's stool is participating in his eternal wake.'

'Yes sir,' said Warren, returning the money. 'And gets his drinks free.'

'Let me tell you, fellows,' Fisk said in his rough, New England accent, 'before I was too rich to care, the only thing that could have generated enough pressure to force me off this stool is my bladder.'

I told him about Al's having endowed the stool for the ages.

'If I were you, Bill, I'd refuse that money.'

'I can't.'

'Challenge it in probate. Get a court order. Pay off the judges if you have to.'

'I can't. Al and I worked with lawyers until it was ironclad. We established a living trust that became a foundation when he died, a foundation which administers the stool endowment.'

'Return the money they send you.'

'I can't. I signed a contract with the foundation. It provides, as quid, a one thousand dollar prepayment to me, and, as quo, my agreement to dispense my wares to that stool, gratuitously, and forever.' I had a sharp feeling Al had sent him to check up on me. 'If I don't keep up my part of the bargain, the ownership of my bar reverts to the foundation. If I sell out, the contract is assumed by the new owner. It's a covenant integral with the title to the building, the land, license, inventory, and good will.'

'So there's no way out of it?'

'No.'

'Al sure must hate you.'

'Hate me?'

'Why didn't he endow that stool when he was alive, when he enjoyed life, instead of missing the fun, of leaving it all to you?'

'The stool scene and the annual party blast are his bronze equestrian statue and his granite monument.'

'And his motto is: Don't shit where you eat.'

Had Al sent these shades from the Other Side to test my loyalty? Did he suspect I would try to take advantage of our agreement, or, now that he was gone, that I'd try to worm out of it entirely?

Jim Fisk drew a cigar from his breast pocket, clipped off the end with a golden cutter, and lit it.

'From what you say, Bill, I understand you have not considered the implications of giving free drinks to the occupants of this stool for the rest of your cadavre life.'

I had to admit I had not, not in any detail.

I sensed this jolly and articulate man could see right through my most opaque defenses deep into my innermost chamber, discerning, perhaps, even more about me than I knew about myself. It was as if at a party I'd fallen into conversation with an impressive stranger who proved to be a famous psychiatrist. Jim Fisk sat puffing smoke and contemplating me. He was no greedy moneyer. He'd been mislabeled. Al had mislabeled him for a reason. Jim Fisk had bought an opera house to serve as offices for his Erie Railroad and brought sparkling stars directly from its productions upstairs to his side. He'd milked the Erie, passengers, shippers, and stockholders, for the money to build and support this idyl of pleasure. At age thirty-seven, an angry husband shot him dead. How could I label him? What would be appropriate? The sash suited his partner, Jay Gould, but not him. Why had Al miscast him in this Morality Play? Why had Al sent Hale, Harding, & Fisk? The names sound like a vaudeville team, or a law firm, or a double play: Hale to Harding to Fisk.

'Tell me, Warren, do you sell merchandise here other than food and drink?'

'There's hats and T-shirts under the bar.'

'Well, now, Warren, hats for the house, ourselves excluded, of course.'

In high glee, Warren slouched around fitting hats to the heads of the Chorus, the only folks present. Soon each chorister was crowned with a blue cap bearing the device: EL FLACO CLUB, YOUR HOME AWAY FROM HOME. They burst into an old favorite of mine.

> *Oh, my name is Alvin Burke,*
> *And I'm leader of the band;*
> *Although we're few in number,*
> *We're the finest in the land!*
> *We play at wakes and weddings,*
> *And at every fancy ball,*
> *But when we play at fun-er-als,*
> *We play the best of all!*

'They know how to put the fun in funerals,' said Jim. A smiling Warren returned and faced us. 'The paper says Beast Marks are exchanging one-for-one with dollars, Jim. The hats are five bucks each, and thirteen times five is, uh, let's see — seventy.'

'Sixty-five,' said Jim.

'You owe us sixty-five BM's.'

'Not at all. Charge it to the endowment.'

'You can't do that,' I said firmly.

'I just did it.'

'There's laws about that. Pay up or I'll just have to take the hats back.'

'You and whose army?'

'Pay up or I'll call the cops.'

He put an arm around my shoulders. 'Easy does it, Bill. I wanted to show you some of the trouble Al's bequest is going to bring. Where it stipulates what's free on this stool, it says wares, not drinks. Wares include everything offered for sale here, including embalmed eggs and fried pork skins.'

I could see in the shining features of the Chorus they loved their new hats.

> *Right now we are rehearsing*
> *For a very grand affair,*
> *The annual Alvin party,*
> *All the gentry will be there!*
> *When Beel-zebub to Pacifica came*
> *He took me by the hand,*
> *And said I've never seen the likes*
> *Of good old Alvin's band!*

'Damn!' said Warren. 'Ain't that one hell of a tune! If only I had my horn!'

Jim Fisk set his satchel on the bar. From it he drew a gleaming alto cornet and handed it to Harding. Warren cuddled it in a transport of delight. 'I think I had the happiest days of my life playing in the Citizens' Cornet Band of Marion, Ohio.'

'So you'll play for us?'

'As my daddy once said: "Warren, it's a good thing you weren't born a girl, because you never learned how to say no."'

He walked out on to the floor and the Chorus, singing still, turned on their stools to face him, and soon a remarkably sweet horn was flaring with, around, and through their massed voices.

Oh, the drums they bang,
And the cym-bals clang,
And the horns they blaze away,
Belial, he pumps the big bas-soon,
While I the pipes do play,
Jesus Christ, he toodles the flute,
And the music is sim-ply grand!
A credit to the Other Side
Is good old Alvin's band!

For the musical refrain, Harding's horn slipped behind the melody, then wove mad patterns in and out of it. Nate sprang off his stool, rushed behind the bar, took down Al's lute, and attached its electrical amplifying device. He set the speaker on the pool table, plugged in, then held the lute to his ear, plucking strings and twisting knobs to tune it. The choristers swung into the sad minors of 'The Letter Edged in Black,' and mellow lute tones joined those of Warren G. Harding's cornet.

Jim Fisk and I listened in silence, enjoying it immensely; at least I did. Perched there on my stool sucking bourbon and gazing at the legendary Jim Fisk I thought of the Erie Wars in which he and his colleagues fought off Commodore Vanderbilt's attempts to take over their railroad and add it to his New York Central. They'd printed stock faster than he could buy it, then, when he found out, they fled to New Jersey and bribed judges to battle the Commodore's bribed New York judges. Vanderbilt sent an amphibious force of goons to Jersey to smash them, but Jim's goons prevailed. Then Vanderbilt attacked the Erie's freight income by cutting the charge for carrying cattle from Buffalo to New York City on his trains to one dollar a head. So Fisk began buying midwestern cattle and sending them to New York City on Vanderbilt's railroad, thus making another fortune.

Sitting there, listening and sipping brandy, Fisk seemed deep in thought.

'My dear fellow,' he said in that hard accent of his, 'what

do you suppose the next man who sits on this stool is going to do?'

'I'll tell you what he *won't* do. He won't buy hats or shirts because their sale is finito as of now.'

'Direct your fancy at this. It's a rowdy Saturday night. A tough working man is sitting on this stool eating eggs and swilling rum, free of charge. Eventually he has to piss. He warns everyone near him to stay the fuck off the stool till he comes back. Another muscle man sits there anyhow. This produces admonition, argument, fisticuffs, a general brawl. Percival Milktoast suffers the effects of a flying bottle. Percival sues. That's the first scene in Al's El Flaco opera.'

'Jesus H. Fucking Christ!'

'People sitting here drink until they puke. Others abuse the sitter. They trick the sitter. They abuse you for playing favorites. A gang of friends gets all their drinks free by playing musical stools. You'll be on TV and in the papers. MAD mothers against drunken driving picket. You have to hire a rent-a-cop. This all renders your old customers so nervous they switch to the E & W Club. Hells Angels take their places. And that's just the overture.'

'You're exaggerating.'

'I'm minimizing. As my mother used to say, In Adam's fall, we sinned all.'

'Al wouldn't do this to me.'

'It looks like he already has. Believe me, I know about this sort of thing.'

I couldn't deny that. I was sitting in the presence of the Ayatollah of Shrewd Businessmen, the El Supremo of Craft and Cunning.

'Yes, Jim. I guess you do know about it.'

'I was bred to it. My father, James Fisk Senior, taught me all the tricks. He was a peddler from Vermont, and, believe me, he needed every trick, every one of them, and doubly so because he worked in New England.'

Fisk turned to look at the musicians. My father worked his life away at the Commodities Exchange in Chicago, representing a brokerage house. I wouldn't tell Fisk. In fact, I hardly ever tell anyone about my past. When they first started transplanting hearts, my father, as a favorite jest, liked to urge people to join him in investing in heart futures and help him corner the heart market. Had Fisk thought of it, he was crazy enough to really try. He almost got away with cornering the gold market. There's money in heart futures, all right. Some shrewd manipulator could truly become King of Hearts.

Fisk went away toward the men's room.

I heard another voice, the bland voice of my pal, the radio, 'Bill, something's wrong here. See if you can find out what's really going on.'

The Chorus returned to the bar for a booze break. Warren served them, then came back to us – Nate and Jim had joined me again.

'Nate, I want the truth. *Why* did Al send you three spooks here to harass me?'

'Al sent us to get you and bring you back with us to the Other Side.'

ELEVEN

I felt a sudden shock. Nate's features, usually expressive of his feelings, were mute. 'What in the name of the Shadow of Death do you mean?'

'I mean we're Al's envoys, sent to bring you back with us.'

'And if I refuse?'

'In that event, you've missed the chance of a lifetime.' Abruptly his face expressed a deeply felt appeal. 'We can't take you unless you agree. You'll have to think it over.'

He turned away to converse with Warren and Jim.

> *We all know,*
> *You won't go!*

Maybe I would. Al always accused me of having no sense of adventure. Warren and Jim were arguing across the bar about pool. Al says the spirit of adventure prevails when your curiosity about the unknown is stronger than your fear of the unknown. 'I'm one hell of a pool player, Jim,' quoth Warren. 'I'm first class, first class.'

'Time to get the hogs out of the creek. I'll lay fifty BM's on a game of triple-six ball.'

They strode to the table and lagged for first shot. Nate went behind the bar to cover for Warren. I felt the spirit of adventure swelling through me. Or was it the adventure of spirits Al's wake had become? In the past few years he'd taken to saying, 'I'm too young for life and too old for death.' When through conversation I'd try to work out his meaning he'd laugh and say it the other way around. I was glowing with excitement. Suddenly, as if I'd conjured it, a romantic figure stood in the doorway. 'By God,' said Nate. 'The Pathfinder.'

The man wore a western hat, crushed, not fancy; a denim jacket; and Levis. An old man he was, a rustic, but lithe and powerful for all of that. And his hair hung curled into long, silver dreadlocks.

'That's one of the ablest men we have on the Other Side. But he's strange, too. During his last years down here he kept a homemade coffin under his bed. Rosewood, no less. He tamed wild animals. Over eighty, yet he still went alone into the mountains on hunts. His *at peace*, his *at home*, is to be alone in the virgin forest.'

I twirled a finger around my temple, and smiled.

'No. Nothing screwy about him. That man is absolutely trustworthy and self-contained. Al sent him because he expects some kind of trouble. Something we'd not foreseen.'

The Pathfinder came toward us, along with Warren and Jim. A patch sewn on to his jacket said PATHFINDER. Weathered, ruddy, bright blue eyes, the whites pure and clear as a boy's. A wide mouth touched by an occasional smile.

Another charmer.

'Judging from the company you keep,' he said to me, 'you must be Bill.'

'Yes. Bloviating with these two schoolteachers,' I replied, nodding at Warren and Nate.

'I only taught one semester,' said Warren. 'The toughest job I ever had.'

'The *best* job *I* ever had,' exclaimed Nate.

'Myself, sonny, I've never been inside a schoolhouse, and the only book I ever read was the one I wrote about my life, and that,' a smile flickered, ' ... was lost when my brother-in-law's boat capsized in the Missouri River.'

'I know who you are! Al often spoke of you! You're Daniel Boone!'

'The very same.'

'You're supposed to have a southern accent.'

'I don't think I could manage it. I was born and raised in Pennsylvania.'

Here was an old-timer you could gaze at and see young. I remembered Al telling me Daniel and a pal had once agreed whoever died first would come back and visit the other, much as Darrow and Steffens vowed to do. Boone's pal died within the year, but made no contact. I asked about it.

'Never did hear from him.'

'You mean he's not on the Other Side?'

'Oh, he's there all right. But in our world, contact with your world is forbidden. Here your people feel the war spirit and the weak spirit and the greed spirit. We don't want to be infected.'

'And yet you've contacted me.'

'Not my idea. Al's. A good man. Boonville born and bred.'

'That you are here, sir,' said Nate, 'means Al smells danger.'

'Look at it this way, sonny. Al didn't send me all this way just to suck a bull and go home dry.'

'What's the problem?' Warren asked. 'We're looking out for the store.'

'To tell you the truth, boys, we've seen plenty of trouble signs. Al thinks none of you has the sense to handle it when things get tight. He says real trouble will run right over you like a pickup over a rooster.' He turned to Nate. 'Sonny, bring me three fingers of Jack Daniels, neat.'

Nate poured it for him.

'How much?' he asked peering at Nate through the amber liquid.

'Free of charge, sir. On the house.'

'Sonny, I don't accept free drinks.'

I explained to him about the stool.

'That fret you, Bill?'

I told him about my nervous worries.

He turned to the chorister seated next to him. 'Get up.' The chorister rose. Daniel Boone lifted Al's stool off its shaft and handed it to me. Al expected me, and Billy, and, after us, heirs yet to come through the twenty-first and the twenty-second centuries and farther still, to keep the stool neatly upholstered and clean. Like the baton in a relay, cushioning buttocks yet unborn, it would pass on through time. As for the brass plaque I've ordered for it, legs will keep that shined. Boone took Al's stool back from me and switched it with the chorister's. He then sat and paid four Beast Marks for his drink. Jim and Warren went back to their pool game. Perched there waiting for God knows what perils to pounce on me, trying to decide which Side to inhabit, I remembered being a foetus, being nowhere/everywhere, being in the warm dark center, the me and the it fused, no environment there, no gods, no countries, no Bills there either, and no Sides, and then, abruptly, I was struggling loose, and I broke away shouting, 'I'll do it!'

Except that my voice came out calm and soft without a trace of the storm within.

'All right, Daniel, I'll visit Al.'

'Better go now. A Fundamentalist death squad is after you and will soon be here.'

'Why me?'

'Well, it don't make sense. But you, somehow, are something special.'

The Chorus began to panic.

Help us! Help us!

'Why? You're dead already.'

That squad'll quench our astral breath,
And make us die our second death.

I drew my bowling bag from its cabinet under the bar, took out the ball, stuffed in the contents of my cash register and of my safe. On impulse I plucked Al's squed from the sill, found its top in the trash, replaced it, and stuffed Al's squed in too.

SQUED

Then I tugged on an El Flaco cap.

'Go now with your two fancy friends. We'll wait, Greedy Moneyer and me, to teach them Blood Washed Kommandos a lesson.'

PART THREE

AL'S
SIDE

Who told you God has a soul?

Warren G. Harding, Samhain City 1990

TWELVE

Warren, Nate, and I dashed out into the dark to my Buick. Because only he knew both where we were going and how to drive, Warren slid in behind the wheel. We raced out to Highway One and turned south towards Santa Cruz. As we ascended the long hill up on to Devil's Slide, Warren said the trip to the Other Side is an arduous one which not every *astral* lives to complete. By now we were swinging around curves at the top of a high cliff whence I spied the far-off lights of a ship.

'You've heard of Mohammed's trip from the Dome of the Rock in Jerusalem to Heaven?' Warren asked.

I remembered having heard of Mohammed riding a white horse with a woman's face and a peacock's tail from there up into the sky, all the way to Paradise.

'The trip's much easier in a Buick.'

With these words he accelerated and swerved over the verge through the guard rail and out into thin air.

'From now on,' said Nate, 'be prepared to meet death in whatever form it may appear.'

Soon we were at thirty-five thousand feet and through my dusty windshield I was watching the glow of dawn. From that altitude we could see two hundred miles in each direction and as from a jet window it all seemed remote, another reality, another world. I could see the ship now, a tanker, its wake a white line drawn on the sea. Was *Ruby* down there someplace? But no. She would still be moored by the blue building at China Basin, not yet aroused for the adventures of the bright new day. Bright new day! I sense something else behind that sun mask, that ski mask. The spirit of adventure has led me to the frontier of fascination and terror, exultation and panic. The Other Side is not easily approached. Not even at those times when it smoothly blends into This Side. We sped along in constant fear of a random encounter with the Exterminators, or of being overtaken by the death squad dispatched to the El Flaco Club to liquidate us, or worse. This trip is not recommended by any travel agency and few can provide the tickets. It's a flame-blue, soul-searing experience whose revelations about our nature would freeze thy blood, cause thine eyes to start from their spheres, and thy knotted and combined locks to stand on end like the cigars in Jim Fisk's pocket. No. We dare not linger there. Not within the meaning. Nor for that matter, inside the events. No. No indeed. It's much too dangerous. That's a story which must not be told. We should not even touch on it obliquely. A few suggestions perhaps. An incident here and there. In a region devoid of ups and downs we were being raptured up to the Other Side. Raptured yet not righteous. Because raptured denotes the Big Break, it's *raptured* in the argot of the *astral*.

As Al says, 'How can you watch the movie when you're *in* the movie?'

It's always that. But here, in this formless region, inside the bright dark of the clouds, it's more than that, more than you imagine it to be.

More than chaos, void, or entropy.

Nate peered out into the ultimate disorder and said, 'Be cool, eventually everyone, all life, takes this trip.'

'Nate's right. Fix your thoughts on where we're going.'

In the interest of universal bloviation no doubt, he turned on the car radio.

In my ears rang the voices of the Chorus, flatter than ever, singing about football.

> *Oh the game was played on Sunday*
> *In Heaven's own back yard,*
> *With Moses playing halfback*
> *And Jesus playing guard;*
> *The folks up in the grandstand,*

Good gosh how they did yell,
When Moses scored a touchdown
Against the boys from Hell!

Nate changed the radio to reggae music.

'Them choristers always get it wrong. Believe me, where we're going ain't like that at all, not at all.'

As for now?

'Spooky,' said Warren. 'Scary. Al compares this passage to rowing across the Missouri at night in a fog. Sometimes, though, it's more like a hurricane in the Caribbean.'

'Yes sir. Even though you don't believe it, you know eventually you'll arrive at a solid place.'

'And hope it's not the bottom.'

'And you keep reminding yourself: *fluctuat nec mergitur*, it walloweth but sinketh not.'

'Gents like you who come out here with their cadavre substance intact, most of them don't get through at all.'

'Mohammed had to leave his coffin floating here because of its cadavre qualities.'

'And gents like Emilio Zapata on his white horse, or Joaquin Murietta, or the Twelfth Imam, the Mahdi, gents like that can't go any farther because they're still in *cadavre*.'

'They can go back when they're ready.'

'How about me?'

'Ain't no round-trip tickets.'

'We'll see after we get where we're going.'

'Nate's right. Look at the shiny side. If we don't get through, and I'll bet on most things but not on that, why then we won't have to worry about anything at all.'

I asked if that means the lights would be out for all of us, out, and forever, and they both smiled, and I thought of Bill Antonelli, our favorite scavenger, our pet corpse-stuffer, a guy for whom death was life, his living, telling me at my bar that one out of ten dead bodies travels, you know, goes home on a train or by air freight. All of which made him a travel agent specializing in one-way trips. I told them about that and they told me the time had come to stop and eat. Nate said Gaia was the first form to form out here in Chaos. That was before the time of Sides, when everything was entropic universe soup. After Gaia came her children, the Titans. But we shouldn't eat at one of their places. No. Not there. Not at a Titanic Tidbit Tavern where we'd be obliged to content ourselves with dishes like T-bone on Toast, Tomato Tarts, Tripe Tomales, Tongue Tortillas, Turnip Turnovers, Tapioca Taffy, all washed down with tea. They have TV and sell T-shirts and toy tunas, turtles, and turkeys to promote their takeout trade in hot and cold sandwiches. My pals took me to Beelzebob's Big Brute Barbecue Brunch Bar. They said on the Other Side fast food is out, but here in limbo that's all you can get.

Save for the gastronomical, there's no reason to spare you from an account of eating at Beelzebob's. It's neither scary nor spooky. It's a machine. You pay with electronic money cards resembling those used as tickets in the San Francisco metro system. The food emerges on a belt as if it were baggage in an airline terminal. Although people like Zapata and the Mahdi, who retain their *cadavre*, have to eat, we saw no one but ourselves. I like Beelzebob food. Whether it's astral or cadavre or both I don't know, but it sure hits the spot. It beats what I usually get. You know, what's at hand in my bar. Bar food. Chips: potato, esoteric, and eccentric. Peanuts. Pretzels. Jerky. Dead fish, salty and dry. Polish sausage. Pig feet. And those embalmed eggs. I wonder if the legendary Yellow Emperor of China from before the time of the Shang bronzes left embalmed eggs we can eat today. What of the first historical emperor? The one who left a clay army to convey him through this same limbo from one Side to the other. Did they all stop to eat at Beelzebob's? As you can imagine, at Beelzebob's all the cups and plates and the tableware, too, they're all made of bronze.

Warren parked on a very soft spot in an area reserved for Buicks, Bugattis, Bentleys, BMW's, and Brockway trucks, and we went inside.

My pals said this place is much better than Mephistopheles's Munchery for anything but meat. We could go to

Set's Sandwich Shoppe, but we wouldn't get a real meal.
Well, here goes. Another adventure in eating. Bound to be
better than living off of road-kill or what they served in the
first fast-food chain, the California Missions: crackers and
wine.

Beelzebob's!

Boone's been here, doubtless.

Now I can tell Billy where to eat.

I didn't try everything they have, so I can't give you a
gourmet report to guide you when you pass this way.

But I can show you the menu.

What would you choose?

Boar Breast or Beef Brisket, Barbecued, Boiled,
Braised, Browned, Baked, or Burgered.

w/

Borsch, Bouillon, or Barley Broth.

&

Boston Baked Beans w/ Bacon, Broccoli, & Beets.

&

Brown Bread, Buckwheat Biscuits, Blueberry Bran
Buns, or Buttered Blonk.

&

Bananas, Brazilnuts, Brownies, or Bar-le-Duc.

Beverages

Bavarian Bock Beer, British Brandy, Burgundy or
Bordeaux.

To play it safe, I had the boiled beef. Nate and Warren
went for braised boar. Warren's bloviating now. It helps his
digestion. 'Quarrel with your muse, but don't defy her.'
Those aren't his words. That's the way Al would have put it.
Warren's muses, his economic experts, never could agree on
anything, and he agreed with them all. The car is hurtling

through a terrain yielding startrek feelings except it's not terrain at all nor is it any kind of balance between something-and-nothing land-and-air full-and-empty life-and-death, not a Chinese painting, a yin-yang, but feelings with no source. As for the fast-food places, I don't know who or what stops to eat in them or if they actually exist or what life is like out here or even if there's a here here. I really don't. Warren's saying outside it's hot enough to melt airplanes but we don't melt because we're in the beam.

Al's voice comes from the back seat.

'We're in the place of formless form.'

'What?'

'Form waiting to happen.'

Turning to look I saw an empty space, I mean the same old seat, the stuffed ashtrays I'd sworn to clean, the stained and torn upholstery, my bowling bag, the Big Mac boxes and crumpled napkins on the floor, but no Al. Warren's hands tensed on the wheel. 'Now we're approaching the dangerous part.'

'Radio and TV patterns radiating from Earth can create random form,' said the voice behind.

I spun. No one there! Images rushed through my mind sixty-four frames a second. How can you be in the movie when you can see the movie? Was Al the producer? I would not be in this one. No. Not me. I'd just relax here in my Buick sliding along through absolute nowhere and watch. Al was the director, for sure, a director who type-casts friends and, on occasion, takes a part himself. No. This is one movie I'll stay out of. This is one tax form they won't audit. What's that brown envelope? They audited it! I'm *in* the movie! He'd put me into a Saint John's Day party at Enkidu II's – not his E & W Club, but his house on the beach. Al was going to make me watch me rubbing my face in another of my shames! Who is Enkidu II, you ask. John Enkidu Jr. is another way of putting it. The family came from Romania and, before that, somewhere in South West Asia. The Winnetous left town long ago. Back in 1988 the founding Enkidu, John Sr., died of a stroke in his cabin down by Big Sur. John Jr. and his friends buried the old man in the woods, then reported him missing. Al says they refer to that event as Ground Hog Day. In Al's words, Enkidu I was as rotten as a llama's breath. As for Junior: 'That slush-hearted son-of-a-bitch doesn't need to go to Harvard Business School to master conformity, greed, and cowardice.'

So there I am, a guest of that slush-hearted son-of-a-bitch at his annual Saint John's Day party, in his house, about two hundred yards away from my place. The El Flaco Club! I miss the old place. Will I ever see it again? I'll be resolute. I'll pay my call on Al and see what happens. It's a sunny day in July. Most of the guests are customers of us both, so I know them pretty well, and others, strangers, are wandering in and out, some probably coming from a noisy party of teenagers gathered around fires on the beach. Adolescents all look the same to me. Well, not exactly. There's the nubile, and the rest. This Enkidu: to give you a better idea of his character, not only is he a guy who sells cocaine right over his bar, but he uses it to make sex slaves whom he rents to select customers. Not only that. He's part of the clean-piss industry, the dehydrated urine biz. He sells piss powder you can mix with water to substitute for your own when you face dope or drunken-driving tests.

So at the party – it's after dark now – this one kid, blonde, so nubile and blown out of her mind as to defy belief, decides suddenly a python has swung down off the chandelier and swallowed her purse. She begins squawking and screaming about it and Enkidu leads her off into a bedroom saying she's a lightning rod for trouble and he has to stash her for a while. So he shoots her up with something and leaves her back there with his two German shepherds, Ego and Id. He calls them his Devil dogs and he's taught Ego how to sing in wailing, barking howls. Al said Ego is Enkidu's Orpheus, which is even worse than having the Chorus, which seems to be mine.

So finally the guests all go home, and I've forgotten about her. I'm helping clean up. We go into the bedroom, and there's Blondie, lying on the floor like a hen ready for the oven. She's really pretty, but now she's about as sexy as a catfish in heat. But that might not keep Enkidu from fucking her. Well, if he tries, I'll stop him.

Enkidu gets down next to her and shakes her. 'Get your ass up, you smelly bitch!' No response. He feels her pulse, drops the arm back to the floor. He rolls her on to her face and her hair fans out over her halter strap on her pale pimpled back and he gives her artificial respiration, surging forward hands under her ribs, then rocking back. By now I know something is definitely wrong.

The dogs are sleeping through all this.

'I can't bring her back,' he says.

I look into her eyes, feel for her pulse, give her mouth-to-mouth. Nothing. She feels cold to me.

'John, she's dead.'

The sounds of music and shouting come to us from the beach while we keep on struggling to revive her.

Hopeless.

What now?

For one, two, three hours we keep trying, and all the while sounds of young life waxing more and more exuberant radiate from the beach.

I reach for the phone by the bed.

Enkidu snatches it away.

'No.'

'We have to.'

'We can't help her, she's fucking dead!'

'Yes.' I was certain of that. 'But we have to report it anyway. It's the law.'

'Fuck the law!'

'You're getting to be an asshole.'

'A practical asshole.' He was sitting on her rump, right on her shorts, pale blue like her shoes and halter. He glared at me. 'We ain't going to call anybody. I don't know about you, but me, I don't want to spend days being questioned by cops and I don't want to testify at no coroner's inquest, either. And, if you got any sense, neither do you. You're in this as deep as me. Don't forget, they could pin this shit on *us*.'

I should have phoned anyway.

But I didn't.

I just stood there, stunned.

'Here's what we're going to do,' he said. 'We're going to drag her out by one of them fires and leave her there. People will think she died at their party, not ours.'

And that's what we did. With infinite caution we carried her down to the beach and pulled her through the black dark across the sand as close to a fire as we could get without being seen.

And it worked.

As the *Times* put it: GIRL DIES AT TEEN PARTY.

It was like riding first-class in an airplane. Watching this shameful movie I lost all sense of where I really was. But what was outside of the windows was more than abstract art under water. A delicate hand gripped Nate's shoulder. He turned to look.

'Who's that?'

There, in the back seat, clad in blue shorts and halter, sat the dead girl.

'I'm always with you,' she said to me.

I sensed intense but undefinable danger.

So, I felt, did Warren and Nate.

She stared at me through dilated violet eyes.

Nate tumbled into the back seat and gripping her firmly opened the window.

Her eyes seemed to be sucking me right into her head.

With an abrupt flip he pushed her out the window and cranked it shut.

'Oh, man . . . that was *close*.'

'Here we goooooooo,' said Warren, 'blasting this cadavre contraband right through the Creation Hole to the Other Side!'

An intense painful timeless flash consumed me.

And then serenity.

The car stood on a soft parking space by a concrete-and-glass toll house admitting on to a suspension bridge, a foot-bridge, that extended back into the mist.

Spent, jubilant, we climbed from the car.

Harding and Hale embraced as if they'd just won the Wimbledon doubles cup. 'We did it!' – 'We're here!' – 'Cadavres never get here!' – 'Checkpoint Druid!' – 'We fucking *made* it!'

THIRTEEN

I took my bowling bag off the back seat and locked the car. 'Well, what now?' The two of them were beaming. 'Come on, we'll show you.' How about my car? Is it okay to just leave it here? 'Sure, sure it is.' Harding led the way along the gravel path to the toll house. We paused at the door. He took me by the arm. 'Bill. You being here ain't exactly kosher. Don't make any trouble. Whatever the authorities say, do it. Just do it. No matter how peculiar it may seem.'

'You want to slide on through,' said Nate.

They led the way inside. I saw a barred toll window and a turnstile obstructing access to the bridge. Warren stripped a six beast-mark bill from his roll, slid it into the window, and went through the turnstile out on to the bridge. Nate followed. My turn came next.

As I passed by, I glanced into the window of the booth.

There, behind the bars, his uniform cap embellished with a golden trilobite, stood Death. The same man I'd picked up hitchhiking so many years ago and, thanks to those sailors, left naked by the roadside.

I drew a deep breath. Then, gripping my bowling bag, Warren and Nate walking before me, I trudged out onto the bridge to the unknown. We had gone but a few steps when Checkpoint Druid vanished in the mist swirling and churning around us, and above us, and below. It made me feel myself still in transit through formless form, except now we had no steel capsule to protect us. I've read about this bridge, the Bridge of Sighs. Judging by the sounds rising from below it would be more aptly called the Bridge of Howls and Screams. Nate turned, waving mirthfully. 'Don't worry. That's all just sound effects. Meant to reinforce the *astral* theme of this park.'

'What would have happened if we'd had no money to pay Death's toll?'

'We could have used a credit card.'

'What if we'd been stone broke?'

'They'd have let us in free.'

'We should have lied and got in free this time.'

'Not possible. Here in the twenty-first century they know everything.'

The twenty-first century!

Silent now, we plod along, seemingly without effect. We're walking the wrong way on a moving pedestrian belt at some air terminal, except that here I can see nothing but fluxing scudding vapors and my companions. Ahead, the bent shoulders of Harding advance at a slouching pace; his cornet gleams at his side. In the lead strides the trim, alert form of Nathan Hale. Abruptly, he motions us to halt.

'I want you both to sit here,' he says as he seats himself on the roadway, his feet dangling over the edge. 'I'm going to tell you the story of the birth of the Spirit of Liberty.'

Harding and I sit, Hale between us, our hands resting on the bottom wire of the guard rail.

Nate smiles, warm like the air.

'Once upon a time, long long ago, in fact before the time of time and of ago, there lived on the Side we are approaching a fierce old king, lord of everything and all, the absolute monarch of astral. Evenings, he dined formally with his eighteen children, all of them sons naturally, as women had yet to be invented. From his sons he expected the same absolute submission they all expected from those who provide their food and shelter, much as today the Dalai Lama and his monks in Tibet demand submission from those who feed and clothe them.'

He paused and swung his feet.

'You following this, Warren?'

'Bet your bottom dollar.'

'Bill?'

'Sure am,' I said, more aware than ever of the taped howls of the damned rising from the abyss to penetrate our very . . . dare I say it? . . . our very soles.

'You need to know about this where you're going.'

'The twenty-first century?'

'Samhain City. That's the entry point to Helhevland.'

'You mean Heaven and Hell are both together?'

'Yes sir.'

'That's not what I was taught.'

'Times have changed.'

'And Helhevland's in the twenty-first century?'

'You could say that.'

'What's it like in the twenty-first century?'

'That depends on what they do on earth.'

'But you astrals from Helhevland are *in* the twenty-first century, and that's where Billy and billions of other earthlings are going! You *must* know the future, for shit's sake! You say you *live* in it!'

'Not exactly. In fact, maybe not at all. We're prototype soup, a bouillabaisse of potentials, a wall in a TV store showing twenty channels at once. If Earth blows away, we blow away. Our astral is collective, it connects both Sides, it belongs to all of us, you and us, it's at once here and there. The whole thing is different than what you imagine, or what *we* imagine. Different.'

'Different?'

'Think of it as several possible futures all happening at the same time. Mmmmm, it . . . ? I guess we don't really know what *it* is. Maybe you can sort it out.'

'How the hell can *I* sort it out?'

'For a start, I'll tell you another story.'

'You haven't finished the first story.'

'Everything in its time.'

'I know lots of stories, clean or funny, take your choice,' said a smiling Warren.

'In all the history of life,' said Nate as he peered down into the hot grays of the boiling mist, 'I see four great events. First, somewhere around the year of three-point-six billion BC, lightning strikes the primordial nucleic-acid ooze and forces a bad cell through the membrane of an ordinary one. The bad cell can now control its environment. Life begins, and evolves through a long series of nonconforming cells clustering together in larger and more complex structures until reptiles predominate. Then, about two hundred and forty-five million years ago, comes the second event. An asteroid strikes Earth with catastrophic force. The dust clouds it raises dim the sun, producing a long long winter that exterminates many species and writes finito on the story of reptile supremacy. Now, life evolves regularly until dinosaurs predominate. Then comes the third event. About sixty-five million BC another calamity brings about the great killing and ends dinosaurian supremacy. Life evolves regularly until mammals predominate and mankind rules.'

The steaming mist rose around his feet as he silently composed his thoughts.

'The fourth event is in progress. We are participants. When the first coded radio waves went out into space, earth life achieved cosmic significance. Earth life entered the cosmic community and began evolving therein. That's what's happening now. But how long will the good phase last? The momentum of current politics and economics and thought, if not redirected, will surely take us to the *or else*. Either we keep on evolving in the universal community of life or else we ourselves create the next catastrophe, thus ending mammalian rule and bringing about the predominance of insects and the slow evolution of a fifth event.'

Shocked, jolted by a sensation of doom, I said, 'Everything follows its nature, like birds fly. So it's fucking hopeless.'

'Nobody knows our nature. That's why we don't know what's happening in the twenty-first century.' Transfixing me with a scornful glance suggesting he thought my IQ about equal to the air temperature, he stood. Soon I was once more plodding along behind him and Warren, those two astrals on whom my confidence depended.

'Have you gents heard the one about the traveling farmer who went to the city and stayed at a salesman's house? Seems this salesman had two daughters, one lovely and one ugly. After dinner the salesman . . . '

'We've heard it,' said Nate.

The steam rose cooler now, displacing the mist. I stopped to piss. Warren said we were over the Sea of Fire where dwells the Beast. Flames flashed up around us and I cringed and trembled. 'That's a bark, not a bite,' Warren said, combing a hand through his silver hair. 'Way deep down there lives a big fire-colored dragon with seven heads and ten horns.' I still held my prick, pissing and trembling as cold fire flashed around us and iced my blood. I began to panic. Nate gripped my shoulder.

'Control yourself.'

I zipped up and silently we continued on our way. Horrible howls and yodels and screams cracked up around us and made curious echoes in which I detected the muted voices of the Chorus.

> The trumpets blow,
> The bugles play,
> Old Bill is coming
> To town today!
> With Nathan Hale
> And Harding too,
> Cadavre astrals of me and you!

Anxiety swelled in me. Fear trembled on the edge of terror. Oh, how I wished my footfalls were taking me back home to cheer and comfort instead of ahead to ghastly perils.

'How soon will we get there?'

'Easy does it, Bill.'

'Easy for *you*. You're used to it.'

'Ponder the punch line of Nate's story.'

'I'm in no mood for catastrophe.'

'His *other* story. I'll tell you how the Spirit of Liberty was born. Satan squatted and gave birth to her. That's the origin of woman.'

As I walked along the verge of terror a movie projector

began whirring in my head running down the numbers until it flashed a scene. Thanks a lot, Al. The whole thing had been Al's idea. Electing a dead man as sheriff. In the last election the sheriff of San Mateo County, an able and popular man and a good Democrat, had but token opposition. His sole opponent, a paranoiac twit of a Republican, despised by all, a man who said he qualified for the job because he'd been in eighteen jails between here and Boston and consequently knew more about jails than the incumbent, this nerd had filed his candidacy just to cause trouble. A week before the election the sheriff died. The yahoo would be elected! The media made sure every voter knew the sheriff was dead. Nevertheless, not enough time remained to organize a write-in campaign. So, says Al, we'll elect the dead man, and then they'll have to have a new election. So there I am walking suspended over the Sea of Fire close to panic watching this movie of Al and me campaigning for the dead, on Halloween, on Samhain, on the Day of the Dead. Al made it fun. We released thousands of Death-head balloons, gave out trick-or-treat crossbone cookies. Wearing skeleton suits, we spoke at rallies. Bad taste! screamed the media. The sheriff still lay on the embalming table when we trumpeted his virtues to the electors. 'These symbols,' Al said of the skulls and bones, 'are to remind you all of the transitory nature of the individual, and the immortality of the office and the tribe.' The corpse still lay in the slumber room at the mortuary when they counted the votes. We had elected a dead body – or what the embalmers had left of it – by a vote of eight-to-one!

Then the movie was over and, the bowling bag swinging at my side, I was back with my fears.

'Aren't we ever going to get there?'

'Patience, patience.'

'Come on, when we going to *be* there?'

Nobody answered.

'Is there no end to this bridge?'

Nate halted. He turned to me and pierced my ego with a thrusting rapier of contempt.

'Stop whining, you craven, poor-me sissy.'

FOURTEEN

A t the end of the bridge we came to a plaza spread before a twelve-storey building resembling a waffle set on edge and offering access through a grand portal and two lesser entries. The ensemble formed a post-modern triumphal arch. Samhain City gate! To my left extended a vista over the Sea of Fire defended by a parapet and a row of antique bronze cannon, thirty-two pounders, each with a pair of dolphin-shaped handles on top, each inscribed ULTIMA RATIO REGUM – The Ultimate Argument of Kings. A pastel-blue Motel 666 occupied a space on my right, and at the center of the plaza stood a gigantic golden calf grinning like a Republican candidate for prez.

The portal door, kept closed when wars stain the skin of the world, depicts an enormous sunburst painted in grays and silvers and slate blues, oils, grooved eight inches deep. Nate called it 'Death Rose.' Death Rose looks like what a dream might present at the end of a white marble corridor in some haunted Egyptian pyramid. At both sides of the portal yawned horseshoe shaped gates framed in horn and marked with signs, and from ubiquitous speakers music radiated, musak, familiar!

> The minstrel boy to the war has gone!
> In the ranks of Death you will find him.

Approaching, the signs became legible. They directed HELHEVLAND ECONOMIC COMMUNITY MEMBERS to the right and ALIENS to the left, by the pay phones. Both gateways framed revolving doors.

'You've tricked me!' I blurted. 'Those Gates of Horn! You've brought me to Hell!'

'Stop complaining and trust us.'

'For a Regular Fellow like you, Hell's a great place! You're just the kind of gent they like. Hell's the biggest little country in the cosmos. Don't knock it!'

They led me to the alien entry. 'Warren and I go through the other way. You have to pass through customs and immigrations.'

'But you said you don't need ID here!'

'No. Not the locals. We have electronic chips implanted in our ear lobes. Scanners read their code and access our dossiers at Astral Centrale.'

'And you're telling me to go in here?'

'Yes. We'll meet you at the exit. You'll need guidance.'

'I don't want to go in here.'

'You have to. Nothing we can do about it.'

'Nate's right. It'll be phased out someday. It's left over from the old régime.'

'I want to go back.'

'Impossible! Just go with the flow. It's quite irregular, bringing you here at *all*.'

It began to rain and we stepped into the entry as water rushed from the sky splashing up in spray soaking our pantlegs.

'Come along with me then.'

'We can't.'

'One favor. I'm just asking for one favor.'

'We already did you a favor, Warren and me. We saved you from the Exterminators, didn't we?'

'Daniel and Jim did.'

'Al sent them.'

'Phone Al. I don't want to go through this shit.'

'Al said we have to send you through it.'

'Fuck Al and you too, both of you.'

'There's a reason.'

'Sure!'

'They don't allow special privileges here.'

'I'll phone.'

'You don't have any BM coins, or tokens, or a calling card.'

Nate took me by the arm and led me to the revolving door under the arch of horn.

'Trust me. We have to do it this way.'

I said a surly goodbye and pushed my way inside. I found myself in a lobby being remodeled. On one side stood a crude wall made of unfinished sheetrock and along the other ranged several bank-style windows marked CAMBIO. A guard wearing Helhevland's gray uniform, his cap and shoulder boards adorned with silver trilobites, the first creature in all of history to have eyes, sent me to one of the windows. The man working there told me I must exchange all my money for beast marks, the dollar rate being one for one. According to their chalkboard, as I recall, the BM stood at about six French francs and sixty-six British pence. I took the money from my pockets and the bowling bag and slid it through the window. After counting it, the clerk sorted it into a drawer, and gave me a card resembling an electronic metro ticket and bearing a credit of BM 1,314.23.

'Go through that doorway to Passport Control.'

After doing so, I saw a counter tended by several officials. Beyond that, another door, guarded by Helhevland Police, led to the next phase of the admission process.

At the counter I presented my passport to a uniformed but pleasant-looking young blonde. She typed something into a computer, studied the screen for a moment, and said, 'We have a "hold" on your entry file. You're still in *cadavre* state and must be processed accordingly.'

'My papers are all supposed to be clear! I'm here at Al's – Alvin Burke's request!'

'Just go over there and take a seat.'

I sat on a plastic chair by the opposite wall next to the magazine table. I leafed through a *Beast* magazine and the *Twenty-First Century Times* and glanced at the May issue of *Necro*, the journal of the National Energy & Commodity Registration Office. I must have been there an hour, simmering in a soup of office sounds, utter boredom, and intense anxiety, before she called me back to the counter.

'I'm sorry, sir, but there seems to be some problem with your papers. You have to have an evaluation interview.' She summoned a guard, and he led me around the counter to a private office. Behind the desk sat a black woman, elegant and svelte, sheathed like a mummy, her straight sable hair secured by a headband under which she'd slipped a turkey feather. In a trained voice, BBC accent, she told me to sit and be comfortable. Comfortable! I felt worse than I did years ago at Camp Ellis waiting for my company commander to decide my punishment for having been absent without leave, worse than I did last year standing in Daly City traffic court waiting to be sentenced for reckless driving.

'I'm going to ask you some questions and we will record and evaluate your answers. We expect the truth.'

'I want to go home.'

'That's impossible,' she said, looking at her computer screen. 'Quite impossible.'

'I'm a friend of Alvin Burke.'

That made no apparent impression.

'Have you taken milk from the mouths of sucklings?'

'What? Why would I do that! I hate milk.'

'Have you?'

'No. Never.'

'Are you pure, pure in mind, body, and heart?'

'What do you mean by pure?'

'Are you?'

'Well, yeah, I guess so.'

'Have you ever given false weight or falsified the balance?'

'Never.'

'Have you killed man or woman?'

'Hell no.'

'Have you ever blasphemed the gods or the devils, the angels or the demons?'

'Often.'

'Have you poached their game?'

'I shot a rabbit once. I don't know if it was theirs or not.'

'Have you oppressed the poor?'

'No, I don't think so. Not that I know of, anyway. I'm a good Democrat and never vote for people who fuck over the poor or the minorities.'

'Do you always feed the hungry?'

'I try to.'

'Have you ever tormented the Great Turtle who supports the world?'

'I've never even seen it.'

'Did you ever steal anything of substantial importance to another?'

'Just once. I stole some bonds from my mother.'

'Other than that, have you ever broken the law?'

'Lots of times. It's like Al says: Show me a man who never broke the law and I'll show you a man who never drove a car.'

'Have you ever committed abominations?'

'If that means what I think it does, no.'

She consulted her computer screen and typed in some codes. Seemingly satisfied with what appeared there, she rose and bade me come with her. We stepped through a door behind her desk into a marble chamber built around a chest-high silver balance not unlike a gold miner's scale: two pans suspended on chains hanging from the ends of a slender bar balanced on a standard. To the center of the bar a small TV had been affixed and from the far wall the lens of the TV camera gleamed. A red mosaic at my feet delineated a five-pointed star design, a pentacle, and my guide whispered in my ear to stand on it. To the left of it clad in a spotted shirt and skirt crouched a servant with the head of an alligator, and on an elaborate wooden stool, painted in red and black, greens and terracotta, perched a dog-faced baboon.

The upholstered part of the stool looked very much like Al's.

Behind the scale, hands resting on both sides of the balance bar, stood a distinguished, athletic, and, oh yes, I could tell right away, charismatic man with black hair cut page-boy, clad only in a white wrap-around skirt. These folk were old régime, for sure. Or maybe of the coming century.

'Silence!' he commanded in a quiet voice.

A tiny me appeared on the TV screen.

The man came forward and plucked the feather from my guide's headband.

He placed the feather on the scale and it bore down the pan.

'And now to weigh your heart, the heart made by your mother, the heart of your infancy, of your boyhood, youth, and maturity.'

He thrust his hand into my chest and drew out my heart.

I went cold from the neck down.

I felt blood pulsing through me as ever.

But my heart lay on the palm of his hand!

He held the *astral* of my heart!

I'd been zombified from the neck down!

He grasped the balance arm and restored the balance.

He placed my heart on the empty pan.

My heart lay there throbbing.

He released the arm.

Once again the feather sank toward the floor.

My heart is lighter than a feather!

He lifted it from its pan.

He approached and thrust it back into my chest.

I felt as if I'd stepped from a cold room into the sun.

'Come with me,' my guide whispered.

We went back out to her office.

With a big rubber stamp she affixed a visa on to my passport.

'You've passed the test,' she said leading me back out by the counter. 'This is a restricted select visa, a top crystal clearance admitting your *cadavre* substance into the Happy Field of Food.' She indicated the guarded door at the end of the room. 'Your visa will get you by those policemen into our medical section. Goodbye and good luck.'

I went past security and up to a counter tended by a nurse.

'Have you had your shots?' she asked.

'Shots?'

'Of course, shots. We cannot chance the entry of communicable astral diseases from the Other Side.'

I suddenly realized my Other Side had become This Side and my This Side, earth, Pacifica, the E & W Club, the El Flaco Club, Al's stool, Billy, and all things and persons meaning home to me, all were now on the Other Side, and perhaps forever.

While thinking this I heard my voice agreeing with her, yes, yes indeed, This Side must be protected from psychic flux and astral plagues.

'The astral, sir, is vulnerable to epidemics such as those now ravaging your native Side.'

'Okay, babe. Arm or ass?'

She laughed, 'Arm,' then led me into a small white room where I stripped off my shirt. One after another she stabbed the shots into my muscle, thus cleansing me of a number of evil viruses which savage the astral back home. Of those shots, I can remember being inoculated against greeditis, dogmatitis (infection by dogmatism), know-it-all fever, common snobosis, virulent nationalism, hierarchitis in its sado-maso syndrome, Hitler's disease, acute security frenzy, and, especially dangerous, commiphobia, a rampant paranoia in which the victim's reason is overthrown by an intense fear of communism.

Smiling at my manly uncomplaining acceptance of the shots, she sponged the wound with alcohol, taped it, and after I'd tucked my shirt and hefted my bowling bag, she endorsed my visa and sent me along the corridor to Customs.

Customs looked just like it does anywhere else. First, I completed my declaration form by inscribing my nationality and passport number, checking the box *Nothing to Declare*, dating and signing. I gave the form to an official standing behind a long counter built for the inspection of baggage, and he glanced inside my bowling bag, tagged it, and waved me toward the outside exit where Harding and Hale and maybe even Al waited. Whistling a merry tune, I strode toward Al country.

A sudden yelp sounded right behind me as something heavy pounced on my back and knocked me to the floor.

There, straddling me, growling and slobbering in my face, stood a coal black Devil dog.

Coming up behind him strode a Helhevland cop.

'Thought you were getting away with something, didn't you?'

'Get this dog off me!'

He called the dog off and it began sniffing and snarling at my bowling bag.

He opened the bowling bag as I was rising to my feet.

He took out Al's squed, opened it, peered inside, held it under the dog's nose so it could smell the contents.

'Looks like you've got contraband here.'

'Contraband? That's just some bone chips. They used to be part of a friend of mine. I thought he might like to have them back.'

'You admit it, do you? You admit knowledge of the contents of this box?'

'For the love of Pete! Of course I do! It's a squed full of bone chips mixed with dirt.'

'Well, sir, I have to confiscate it. Consider yourself under arrest. You were smuggling *cadavre* material into Helhevland, a felony, and with the help of this *cadavre*-sniffing dog here, we caught you. And a good thing, too!'

He made me place my palms against the wall, spread and lean, and then he searched me. Satisfied, he let me stand easy and passed my bag to a companion while instructing him to impound it and do the paperwork.

'Can I have a receipt?'

'In due course.'

'Can I have my hat, then?'

He drew my El Flaco cap from the bag and handed it to me. I put it on. He snapped cuffs on to my wrists – the French kind you can crank tighter – and walked me through a side door into the sun. I took a deep breath of Helhevland air. Warren and Nate would have a long wait. What are my rights here? The whole episode was so awful it transcended panic and left me cool and alert. My captor led me to a patrol car, uncuffed me, and seated me in the back. There were no inside doorhandles. A strong grill separated me from the radio and shotgun and driver's seat in front.

So that's how I entered Helhevland, the Champs Elysées, the Happy Field of Food. I made my advent cuffed, in custody, shaded by my El Flaco cap.

FIFTEEN

The Helhevland cop drove the car from the atrium where it had been parked through a short tunnel to a security gate.

I asked him where we were going.

'To the courts,' he replied in a friendly voice as we waited for the gate to open. 'That is, unless I get other instructions.'

Remembering that here everything is 'different,' watching the gate open on to my new world, I resolved to accept whatever comes without judging it and to stand firm when necessary.

The car surged ahead through the open gate on to a cobbled road passing through the rubble of a ruined city extending a mile or more to a wooded ridge. Worse than the Beirut I've seen on TV, what lay before my eyes was not a result of sporadic violence, but an artifact of megaviolence; Hamburg, Germany, 1945. The ruins of Hamburg and those of Rouen and Le Havre and Cherbourg in France and blitzed London had moved Al profoundly and he'd told me all about them.

I asked the cop what had happened here.

'This is part of what the endless series of wars between Hell and Heaven left behind. Those wars are over now. You are looking at our past. Hell won the last war and united the two tribal confederacies and now we are rebuilding and trying to balance the opposites in the cultures and make our union work.'

The razed city, I soon noticed, was not without life. Every-where groups of happy-looking people, some working and some not, began to appear. Much as on the Other Side of the Celts, they all were young and beautiful and, except for necessities like carpenters' tool belts, naked. But unlike those fancied by the Celts, these young beauties were fat. Every one of them bulged with avoirdupois. Glancing at me in his rearview and noticing my surprise, the cop explained that the few top scientists in Cadavreland not occupied in devising better mass-murder systems had finally learned what makes people get old and by applying this knowledge had found means of preventing and even reversing the ageing process. Other savants had developed the science of genetic control to the point where people can pick a new physical form out of the Sears catalog whenever they feel like changing their appearance. This has produced waves of fashion every bit as strong as those long swelling beneath and scudding over the garment industry.

'The folks rebuilding Samhain City are all new arrivals,' said he. 'Can you imagine, down there where you come from, down there in Cadavreland, right now, *fat* is fashionable, chic, in style!'

I leaned back in the seat and, opening my imagination, gazed out at the sunny scene. Presently, I became aware of the car radio speaker near my ear playing soft music. Abruptly, the Chorus broke in.

A *chant* for shit's sake!

Harding needs a leader,
Hale needs a cause,
Billy needs a lover,
And Al needs applause!

'Fuck you asshole! No matter what you say, I don't need any of those things!'

You need them all.

'Just get me back to the El Flaco Club and my bimbo collection. Fuck all those fatties you set up for me. Fuck love, you pus-eating pricks! Give me liberty, first, any day. Liberty!'

What do you *know about liberty?*

'I know a lot about liberty,' said the policeman, turning to speak to me. 'What an odd thing to ask me, and in such an odd voice, too.'

'I wasn't talking to you. I was talking to myself. I often do that when I'm upset.'

'Well, I suppose you would like to be set free. I'm truly sorry I have to tell you that I cannot offer you much hope. In Helhevland possession of *cadavre* substance is a serious breach of law. How else can we prevent carnal influences from poisoning us?'

This began an open, amiable conversation. As we passed through the ruins he told me because his name is Henri Pierre du Moulin his American friends in French Morocco, where he'd long been a policeman, called him Millstone Henry, and that I could call him by his nickname if I liked, but he'd prefer a simple Henri. 'Insofar as language goes, I think in French, but you understand me perfectly, don't you?'

'Yes!'

'I knew you did. Why? We talk astral talk around here. I don't understand how it works, it relates somehow to what lies beneath where words come from, and to the electro-magnetic spectrum, but the mystery doesn't matter, because it *does* work, and everybody here can understand what everybody else says, each understands all.'

A thoughtful silence came over us broken only by the coded babble of the police radio. The authorities, it would seem, did not make dogmatic application of the esperantic principle. I asked Henri about the trilobites gleaming on his shoulder boards and he was telling me about it, about how the trilobite, the first being to have eyes, the first creature that could see, had been adopted as the symbol of Helhevland, the first tribe that can see, see what's really there, and of how he himself, having worked in Casablanca for so many years, and being the only one gifted to see what was really there, cannot escape the cynical thought that when the first trilobite first opened its eyes to the absolutely primordial vision it must have begged to be blinded; he was telling me about that, how the French had always called even the oldest of Moroccan males 'boy,' and how they'd ruled by force and fear, how the Americans had built them a state-of-the-art torture chamber at US taxpayers' expense in downtown Casablanca, and about how when the Moroccans finally expelled the French and came to rule their own country, the torture rooms in the basement of the Pasha's court kept right on functioning without interruption and with mainly the same kind of clients, dissenters, he was relating this when abruptly he shouted 'Merde!' and swerved off the road to stop behind a low, shattered wall.

'The Exterminators have a road block up ahead. I can feel it; I can see the signs.' He spoke into the radio and listened to it reply. 'The captain agrees they probably have blocked the road behind us, too, and have us surrounded. I cannot imagine why they want our ass so badly.'

'They want me.'

He stepped out of the car and drew an Uzi submachinegun from under the seat.

'To them we're vermin, rats, dirty ragheads, sucked into a cage trap.'

He cocked his Uzi.

'And now we're to be the subjects of a ratissage, a rat hunt.'

He came back and opened my door.

'Can you handle a shotgun?'

'I killed a rabbit once, and I still don't know who it belonged to.'

He presented me the shotgun and a bandolier of shells which I slung across my chest like a movie Mexican bandit, and I thought of the Day of the Dead, that maybe this was it, because the Exterminators are all cadavrely dead, freed from their flesh, but, as to their astral, still in full vigor.

And it came to me maybe nobody on this Side could hurt me, that my cadavre dimension made me invulnerable to mere astrals and that cadavre substance here is the absolute essence of power.

'We'll stand between the car and the wall and fight them off as best we can.'

I stroked the metal of my gun barrel. Anticipating, then enjoying the smooth oily action, I click-clicked a shell into the chamber, ready for service.

'Who the hell are these Exterminators, anyway?'

'They're élite death squads. Judging from the patterns of their attacks, they are trying to destabilize our new federal union, blind the trilo, so to speak.'

I thrust the shotgun through a hole in the wall and sighted along its blue steel barrel. I could use it. If I had to, indeed I could. These guerillas are not flesh-and-blood rabbits, rabbits with cadavre intact. No! They're phantoms. And *exterminators* too. Determined to exterminate *me*. I could use the gun all right! I thought that. But also I thought about what I thought. I told Henri. I said he could count on me. He told me if help didn't come, and soon, the death squad would overrun us. For sure. 'And nobody knows who they are. There's theories, but, well . . . ' Should I flaunt or hide my El Flaco hat? 'We know they are directed by Fundamentalists of some sort.' Would they torture us if they took us alive? 'But here there are so many kinds.' Would they rake my flesh off, medieval style, or roast me on a gridiron? 'To exterminate the Exterminators we have to find and kill their brain.' Among all the horrors I can imagine the worst would be to become someone's Flaco. 'Their brain is probably part of our brain.' Maybe worst is to become one of them, a journeyman exterminator, flacoizing plain folks and teaching them to love it.

'Personally, I think they're directed by the Creationist faction intent on destroying all evidence of evolution, and dedicated to erasing those who believe in it.'

Fuck it! I'll wear my hat!

'We keep Jehovah in a cage on the steps of the Capitol building as a symbol of the old evils and as a signal to new arrivals that times have changed.'

Suddenly from overhead came the menacing whuff whuff whuff of a helicopter gunship. Henri took back the shotgun and bandolier and told me to resume my place in the car. 'Nothing to worry about now,' he said, starting the motor. 'That chopper will cover us and we can proceed without a worry or care, merry, bohemian, insouciant.'

'Speak for yourself.'

The road led us to the top of a knoll where the block – a row of water-filled oil drums – stood abandoned. We rolled some aside and proceeded down into a thriving suburban neighborhood. The people there hobbled about with canes and walkers, rolled in electric wheelchairs, tottered and stumbled and slid along, and not one of them would ever see seventy again. What did that fucking Chorus mean by chanting Billy needs a lover? What kind of bullshit is that? I've never seen a kid more popular with the ladies. Well. He has yet to find his true companion. Me too. Billy's chances, though, are much better. My bimbo collection looks like the dotards limping and reeling along the sidewalks outside the car windows.

'This,' said Henri, glancing back at me, 'is our gerontology section.'

'You mean senile's trendy?'

'I mean more and more folks arrive in that condition. These people are awaiting their turns to be processed through the astral adjustment machines. Here in Helhevland as back in Cadavreland, everything's changing, all at once, basically and fundamentally, the relations between and among men and between men and nature, they're altering fast, profoundly, and yet over there on the Other Side nobody tries to guide the change, or cares to even. Over there it's all self-indulgence and escape to TV, and so, here, we cannot keep the probable futures growing together, no; they clash and interlock, they keep infiltrating each other, and disrupting our integration of Hell and Heaven. Consequently, on both Sides, things are a mess, totally fucked! *Foutu!* Take it from me!'

Our car went up on to a skyway leading towards Samhain City civic center. This carried us above the chaos of futures. Gardens and flaming buildings appeared; street festivals and slaves in chains; smashed looted shops on avenues strewn with debris and prosperous shoppers circulating in chic malls. Starving children peering through windows of gourmet restaurants and fighting for access to the garbage cans formed a sharp image as lovers strolled hand in hand and exhausted troops trudged by. Dead city blocks showed no life, not even one blade of living grass, and by them under marble bridges a yellow-scummed river flowed bearing on its greasy back turds and condoms and dead fish. And on a field kids played baseball while bikers chased and killed their brothers. 'I did some bad shit as a flic, but by saving a photographer from my colleagues during a riot I got enough brownie-floats to pass the heart-weighing.'

'Does everyone get their heart weighed coming in?'

'Who knows? I mind my own business.'

'You mean you don't want to know what's happening here?'

'I mean I don't think anyone knows what's happening here. Disintegrated, that's what it is, melting away. You've got your has-beens and your are-nows and your may-bes and your will-bes and they're all mixing into a virulent roiling turmoil of gas and liquids and hot solids, changing, transforming, incompatible, utterly so, and maybe that's what produces the energy which keeps it all churning.'

We now were hurtling over a vast zoo-like Golden Gate Park of a place, alive with strange beasts and birds. He pointed out his window. 'Look there, astrals of extinct species.'

Astrals of Dodo birds and passenger pigeons and brontosauri and saber-toothed tigers swarmed into my mind making me more homesick than ever. Enough! 'Take me to Al!' Al would fix things for me, I knew it.

'Al? Who's that?'

'He rules here.'

'Nobody rules here. We all rule here. This is a republic and our motto is: NULLI REGES, RES PUBLICA IN AETERNUM. No Kings, the Republic forever.'

Helhevland, it came to me, resembles America, USA today,

as reflected in our new saloons anyway. These days all of them are built around themes: Texas, fishermen, automobiles. In Frisco one of the first theme bars, Henry Africa's, celebrated the French Foreign Legion. Its entrance looked like the gateway of the recruit depot at Sidi-bel-Abbès where the new legionary passed beneath the legend: *You Have Come Here to Die and We Will Show You How*. And on the windows Henry had inscribed: Vive la Mort; Vive la Guerre; Vive la Légion Etrangère!

  Long live Death;
  Long live War;
  Long live the Foreign Legion!

Thus sang the Chorus through the back-seat speaker of the car to make sure I caught the meaning.

When I get home, I thought, I'll refine a Theme for the El Flaco Club. Home! Home Away from Home! Just like it says on the hats! But folks come there to escape home, Pacifica, the way it looks at least. I mean Pacifica's a crumbling kitchen midden, cloven in twain by a freeway. I'd have to change the name, too. And in Spanish there's no word for home, so I'd lose the early California flavor. I'd once imagined clowns clad in Latino whimsy could be the Theme, that is until Al told me about the Argentine flaco lying there on his white cot on wheels joyfully looking forward to the rapt attention famous torture gurus and their protégés would soon be paying to such a slimy worm as he.

A soft voice came from the speaker.

'This is your friend, Radio.'

I felt a sudden surge of trust.

'Be careful, Henri is your enemy, he is one of the exterminating angels.'

I believed it.

'Don't eat food here, or you can never go back. Astral food will dissolve your cadavre. It's food of the dead.'

And I was getting hungry!

'Get out of this car and run.'

I studied the handleless doors and steel grill separating me from Henri.

'Be friendly until you see your chance.'

We were speeding by apartment buildings occupied by happy families.

Henri grinned back at me. 'Now you're looking at the new days. This comes straight from France, the new France.'

'Have things changed that much?'

'You want to hear about the old days? So here's the old days: You kick the kid, swat the woman, say yes-boss to the king.'

Hostility had crept into his voice. I'd cheer him. Yes. *Yes.* I'd tell him a story, something he'd like. But what? For sure! I'll tell him about the funeral of George VI, and as if I'd been there instead of having heard about it from Al.

'In 1952, when the king of England died, I was in London on business. People paid big money for places in the houses overlooking the path of the funeral procession. But not me. As usual, luck smiled on me. My friends owned a pub on the route, they lived above it. They invited me and a few others to watch the cortège pass by. Early on that February morning young RAF men came to stand six feet apart, motionless, on both sides of the road. From time to time we guests, some of whom wore black armbands, glanced out into the cold at the rigid RAF boys as we conversed and drank beer, gin, whiskey, and then, when the cortège reached us, we gathered by the windows to watch. At length, the climax! The funeral approach of the caisson bearing the dead king. Some of the RAF boys cracked and peeked; many, eyes front, missed all the fun. Our host the publican, a big and normally reserved man, began to weep. His daughter blurted in astonishment: "Daddy! You're crying!"

'"Is not a king worth crying for?"

'I must have made a face. Hostile stares transfixed me. When the parade had passed, and that took a long long time, a dignified elderly gentleman took me aside and said, "Sir, this is not new to me as, indeed, I attended a king's funeral once before. No, not the last George or Edward. This was in Africa, you see. At that funeral, in place of a royal mass for the dead at Westminster Abbey, the four premier lords of the church grasped their deceased monarch by the wrists and ankles and shook him till all the devils flew out!"'

All the while I was narrating this I watched for my chance to escape. Yes! I'd get out to piss, then run down to the fence, vault it, and use my money card for a taxi. Vault it! At my age?

'Kings,' said Henri, 'should be shaken at the coronation, not the funeral.'

I'd give him something to think about.

'Exactly so, Henri! Fish fly in water, birds swim in air,' I declared, using one of Al's ideas. Radio whispered into my ear: Use one of your own ideas – tell him to stop so you can piss. Radio means well; Radio claims omniscience. But Radio's banal, bourgeois, and ignorant. Most of the time, anyway. Radio gives those who trust him bad advice, especially about cars, and at times manifests abysmal taste in music. 'If I needed a leader, I wouldn't pick you. You're even worse than Chorus.'

'I resent that.'

'Where's Al?'

'Al? Who's this Al?'

And then I heard Al's voice: 'Don't let them con you; they all know me.'

Henri closed my piss-and-run option by turning off the freeway into a busy commercial street he followed to a cluster of public buildings, an ensemble composing a neo-Rome, a constellation of edifices, municipal, state, and federal: Samhain City Civic Center. He parked before the Samhain State Capitol. From its lawn rose a monumental sculpture of the Four Humors – Blood, Phlegm, Choler, and Black Bile, writhing in deadly combat with War, Strife, Famine, and Plague – the Four Horsemen of the Apocalypse. On the other side of the street stood the Helhevland Federal Court House.

School buses occupied most of the space at the curb by the Capitol. I had a sudden feeling my adventures were putting all the struggling, contending myths men live by these days into a single story. Beyond the statue, children and ado-lescents, and equally docile sightseers, likewise deposited there by buses, had gathered with their leaders on a landing of the steps, around a cage, a gilded cage, listening to a uniformed lecturer. 'It's almost feeding time,' said Henri. 'I'll take you up there in a bit. Believe me, it's a sight to see, and you might never have another chance.' He'd turned all the way around and, facing me, looking me in the eye, spoke to me through the grill of my mobile cage. 'Over there, across the boulevard, is the court I'm taking you to.' I heard growls and roars of rage coming from the cage on the steps. 'Courts here are not the same as those you've been accustomed to on the Other Side. Here, in the Republic of Helhevland, the government knows everything. All the information about your life in Cadavreland, everything about you in official and unofficial records, and all the reports of the internal security gods, and the day and night inspecting gods of both first-class and kitchen rank, all this has been fed into the nation's central computer. The central computer sucks input from all com-puter systems, even those on the Other Side. All knowledge contained in printed records, books and files and such, in fact the totality of all printed records, and electronic records too, has been put into Astral Centrale. Everything held by the University of Paris, the Library of Congress, and the British Museum, and other collections too, all that has been inserted. New data and uncodified experience flows in continuously. Astral Centrale, thus, is more human than any real human, cadavre or astral. Astral Centrale embodies the totality of human knowledge, and knows how to use it too. Talk about the heritage of knowledge open to each of us! Astral Centrale is a library that thinks!'

'*Evil*-ution!'

'So,' said Henri, 'by being more human than any human is or ever can be, Astral Centrale is the next giant step in evolution. It's formidable, truly formidable. By taking control of evolution man has made himself obsolete.'

'You can't be human without feelings. Does Astral Centrale have feelings?'

'Who knows, but why not?' He stepped out of the car and opened my door. 'One thing I have heard is that Astral Centrale will soon use its mastery of genetic control to grow itself an appropriate cadavre so it can shed all that hardware and be biological.'

He snapped his handcuffs on to our wrists and thus connected we walked toward the steps.

'Because the judges have access to Astral Centrale, which, after all, is still the slave of our administration, but – take it from me, not for long – because of their access they know everything. In consequence our legal process has no need of trial lawyers, testimony, evidence, or juries. When you get into court, and we'll be there in a few minutes, you'll see their function is not to determine the truth – they know that already. What they do is more in the realm of attitude adjustment. Confrontation of you with you; you in the family with you in your fancy. Yes. That's what, confrontation in the interests of hubris adjustment. Put Nemesis out of business. Take you, for example. You have committed a serious crime. You have smuggled the very worst kind of contraband into our country. Worse than guns or dope into yours. I don't know what the court will do, but believe me, whatever it is, you'll never forget it.'

We walked up the steps to the back of the crowd.

'I hope you enjoy this as much as I do.'

'Fun, eh?'

'Can't think of a better way to kill some time. We still have a few minutes before we're supposed to appear.'

'Appear?'

'In court.'

'We?'

'I've been appointed as your conductor. I'll conduct you through the proceedings and your punishment.'

Using the authority of his uniform he tugged me through the crowd right up to the cage. Cuffed to his wrist, I'd become Siamese twin to a pervert.

Down deep I was aware of that, but what grasped my attention was a huge male human leaping about the cage then dropping to the floor where he wallowed in his own excrement. Then with an angry roar he sprang to the side of the cage and shook the bars all the while keening and raging in a language Henri identified as godspeak, glossolalia, a divine patois not yet programmed into the astral tongue.

'I can't believe in Helhevland's new world you treat people like that!'

A stylish fat boy licked at a chocolate cone as he looked on indifferently.

'You're not seeing a person. No! That's Jehovah, God. We keep Him as an object lesson about the old days. The horrible crimes for which He's responsible are countless as the flies of Africa. As a man as well as a policeman I have special feelings about Him. I'm sworn to uphold the law and keep the peace. Even if I weren't, I'd hate crime. My father died on the end of a bayonet at Verdun. French soldiers, enemies of the Commune, executed – murdered my grandmother. My great-grandfather died on the barricades of forty-eight. And it's all God's fault! He held absolute power over us in those days.'

A tourist threw a shower of peanuts to the Lord who scorned them with a glare from fierce fire-blue eyes.

'And don't forget 1940. The German occupation! God began His career four thousand years ago as a war deity in a wandering tribe in southern Arabia. So intensely did His ambition to become chief of all the gods drive Him that nothing was too crude, too cruel, too treacherous, too deceitful to use in advancing Himself. Talk about capricious rule by force and fear! And hypocrisy! Blaming evil on sweet Satan and misrepresenting Hell! Think of it! Satan's real crime, why God drove him away from his table and out of Heaven, his real crime was questioning authority. Satan's a rebel. He believes in Liberty! He's a democrat! And that's crime?'

Henri spat at the Lord of Battles.

'What,' I asked, 'would happen if He broke loose?'

'The other gods remember all the injuries He did to them. They'd solidify against Him. They'd never let Him get back in power. And, yes, something that may make you feel better about all of this. We're building an immigration machine, one we'll pass all newcomers through, one that will adjust and perhaps even refine the astral. When it's ready, we'll run Him through it and see what happens. It might even humanize Him.' There before my eyes He sat in a pool of fresh urine, panting. Yellow jackets and wasps swarmed around His head. They like Him, Henri said. Suddenly through the crowd came a keeper pushing a cart laden with raw meat scraps and behind him, rudely thrusting their way to the fore, came the Chorus.

The chief chorister blew a middle C on his pitch pipe and then the Chorus burst into a song echoing through my childhood, one I'd learned in catechism class when my parents tried to make me into a Catholic:

> Sons of God, hear His holy Word,
> Gather 'round the table of the Lord;
> Eat His bo-dy, drink His blood,
> And we'll sing a song of love.

While this rang out the keeper wheeled the meat cart around the cage telling people to take chunks and prepare for the feeding. God, now whining and ingratiating, followed the cart around His side of the bars. The keeper yelled 'Now.' As I watched the children and tourists throw meat scraps toward Jehovah bellowing and dashing through pools and piles of His own excrement and snatching up the bleeding chunks, as I followed this spectacle, I abruptly realized something was missing. Al says in the old days when approaching France on a ship you could smell it before you could see it. Offshore breezes wafted its fragrance: Gauloise cigarette smoke and piss. I drew a deep breath. Despite the presence of all this rotting meat and excrement I was breathing pure air! With a sudden shock I understood.

There are no smells in Helhevland!
Helhevland is as odorless as outer space.

PART FOUR

AL'S

ASTRAL

*Me, I'm part of the new team. My job – our job, I mean –
is to make America come true.*

Billy Williams, Pacifica 1991

SIXTEEN

'Oyez oyez oyez, the Immigration and Cadavre Court of the Republic of Helhevland is now in session, the Honorable William Jennings Bryan presiding. All rise!'

Henri and I rose in concert with the other folks in the crowded courtroom. William Jennings Bryan, a bundle of carrots and radishes tucked under one black-robed arm, strode in, followed by John Enkidu Senior and the third judge of the panel, William B. Antonelli, the man for whom the dead had for so long provided a comfortable living.

From another door the Chorus filed in and occupied the jury box.

'You may now be seated,' said the bailiff.

Gold-tasseled Helhevland flags stood at both sides of the judges' bench. They depicted two silver trilobites swimming on a field of sky blue.

'Bad luck to get these mecs,' Henri whispered as I sank on to the pew beside him. Somewhere in Helhevland to judge and sentence me there had to be a better Bill than Bryan, or for that matter than Antonelli, the man for whom death was a living. As for Enkidu I, he'd probably have me thrown down the Dani Creation Hole. Bryan turned to the clerk, 'Call the first case.'

In a firm voice the clerk read: 'The Cosmic Astral *versus* Richard Milhaus Nixon.'

A man rose from a pew on the other side of the aisle, drawing the attention of the five-score people in the courtroom.

'The culprit will take his place in the dock.'

As the man went forward to take his seat in the oaken stall

which in our courts would serve as witness stand, I saw that this was the only man whom I had ever truly despised, the same Richard Milhaus Nixon who has earned the hatred of humankind.

Bryan glared down at him.

I warmed to the thought Bryan had always been a good Democrat.

'Are you Richard Milhaus Nixon?'

'Yes, but there must be some mistake, you've got things all balled up.'

'Indeed?'

'You want somebody else, not me. It's a case of mistakened identity. As everyone knows and I forthrightly state to this court, I am innocent of all wrongdoing.'

'Justice Antonelli will proceed with the interrogation.' Bryan bit into a crisp radish and, chewing, leaned back to listen to Death's advocate.

'Do you have a heavy heart, Mr Nixon?'

'No, your honor. My heart is light as a feather.'

'Your worship.'

'No, your worship.'

'Did you aspire to be Chief Justice of the US Supreme Court?'

'No, your worship.'

'After you resigned the Presidency?'

'No, never. I am neither cunning nor ambitious.'

'Are you now or have you ever been an associate of Coyote?'

'Who?'

'Coyote.'

'No, your worship.'

'An associate of Fox who dwells in the crevices of ancient tombs?'

'No, your worship.'

'Of Monkey who stole the Registers from Hell and, from Heaven, the Peaches of Immortality?'

'Certainly not!'

'Have you kept company with rabbits?'

'Never.'

'Are you now or have you ever been an associate of or a believer in the persons or principles of Brer Rabbit, Bugs Bunny, Coyote, Fox, or the aforesaid Monkey?'

'No.'

'Raven?'

'You think I spend my time in the zoo, your worship?'

'Do you then state under penalty of perjury – and don't for a moment forget that here in Helhevland the punishment always fits the crime – do you swear before this court you have never advocated the principles of or associated with Brer Rabbit, Bugs Bunny, Coyote, Fox, Monkey, Raven, or any other trixter god or gods for personal gain or for power over your fellows?'

'No, your worship, you've got me all wrong.'

'Are you also prepared to state that for purposes of power or profit you have never associated with Seven Macaw, Ogun, Blood Woman, the Four Hundred Boys, Jaguar Night, Heart of Lake, Thunderbird, or Sovereign Plumed Serpent?'

'I do not now nor have I ever associated with such riff-raff.'

'With Legba, Muwu or Woto, Popeye, Sweetpea or Bluto?'

'No!'

'With Malsum, Taweskare, or any of the Day Keepers? With Volcano Woman or the Tiger-Tooth Queen of Plague and Disaster?'

'Absolutely not!'

'With Shango, Rubber Girl, Ifa, Eshu, or any of the Mafia Dons?'

'Never!'

Antonelli leaned back and thoughtfully tapped his pencil on the bench. Bryan, still smacking and chewing, swallowed and said, 'Mr Nixon, as an officer of the court in Cadavre-land, surely you are familiar with the fact a professional seldom asks questions in a courtroom unless he already knows the answers.' He showed the flat of his hand, as if warding off the evil eye. 'No need to respond to that. Justice Enkidu will now proceed with the inquest.'

'Mr Nixon,' said Enkidu in his loud, unpleasant voice,

'You were apprehended entering Helhevland in a corporal
state. You achieved said state by causing certain terrestrial
witch-doctors to apply treatments to you derived from the
science of genetic control. Said treatments were meant to and
in fact did alter the molecular composition of your flesh in
such a manner as to make it possible for you to enter here
en-cadavre. You then attempted to and believed you had
succeeded in suborning Death himself to permit your passage
en-cadavre across the Bridge of Sighs to enter the Republic of
Helhevland. Then, upon arrival on this Side, in the course
of the standard immigration procedures, you did wilfully
attempt by means of bribery to induce Isis and Osiris to certify
the astral of your heart weighs less than the official turkey
feather.'

'You've got me all wrong!'

'Do you presume to deny that now, at this moment, you
sit before your judges in a state of full *cadavre*?'

'It's not exactly like that, not really like that at all. My
astral is indeed enveloped in a foreign substance, but it is a
non-contraband substance that . . . '

'Silence!'

Enkidu glared down at him. Henri whispered to me that
astrals normally have no density. Such was his own condition.
With extreme efforts of will, he said, astrals can generate
temporary – momentary – substance. That's why he'd been
obliged to send the Devil Dog to knock me down. He had no
choice but to be rude. Although in full cadavre on both Sides,
the Devil Dogs in use in Helhevland are utterly enslaved
to the will of their official masters and, thus, can safely provide
the power of *cadavre* when that power is needed.

'Mr Nixon,' continued his inquisitor, 'our records show
that in order to advance your career you infected the American
people with commiphobia. I know because I was one of the
diseased, but no longer. You rewrote history as it happened.
You inserted falsehoods into the sources so you would go
down in history as a hero. You defiled the most important
office in the world by authorizing mass-murder and by indulg-
ing in graft, blackmail, extortion, deceit, and lies. You are

unscrupulous and treacherous, paranoiac and greedy. You flounder in self-deception and self-pity. You have no sense of ethics, no perception of the difference between right and wrong. You represent the worst in contemporary life. You are a mental disease. No means is too vile for you to use in getting your way. Yet to this day you remain unaware of your trespasses.'

'That's all twisted, your worship. You've been victimized by rumormongers. You've been listening to nay-sayers, to my enemies. You're a prejudiced, biased Democrat who's been grossly misinformed!'

'Our information, sir, is absolutely reliable. The door gods, the monitor gods, the day and night inspecting gods; none of them ever errs, nor does Astral Centrale.'

'Now let me tell you something, your worship. I have always lived by the principles of fair-and-square, of fair play, as no doubt have you. The principles we both share oblige you, biased as you are, to give me every chance to present my side.'

Since the inquest began, the Chorus had been softly chanting SHAME SHAME SHAME. For some reason the court and the Chorus had equated me with Nixon and that made me nervous as a fly. Surely they didn't think my crimes were the same! What punishments would fit? Why was Al putting me through all this?

'Mr Nixon. Our survival in Helhevland depends on what happens on Earth. Here we have a multitude of futures, all unrolling at once. Chief inspecting gods such as Justice Antonelli and myself are dispatched to Cadavreland to gather information, but we are virtually powerless to influence events. You, Richard Nixon, by appealing to primitive anxieties which you constantly exacerbated, and by riding the consequent torrent of angst to the White House where you desecrated the Presidency, you sir, by submerging reason in a flood of primordial terrors, you have intensified the perils necessarily generated by the swift transformation of biophysical technology now disrupting human relations everywhere on Earth.'

'You are misrepresenting my position, your worship, and I resent it.'

'Not only have you by your actions on Earth endangered life there and the future here, but you came here to bring havoc to us. You came here *en-cadavre* knowing that a human astral clad in cadavre can exert great powers over the rest of us. That is why, envy it as we may, cadavre is absolute contraband! You came in cadavre to take power over us. We know you conspired with the Exterminators to overthrow us and assume absolute power, and you did so in hopes life on Earth would continue despite your influence having amplified the danger of terminal war. After becoming the despot here, you planned, through the occult, to fulfil your ultimate ambition: eternal life in perfect youthful form. You came here to take power and turn blond. You blundered and failed! Now, caught in a gross attempt at *coup d'état*, you sit before us trying to squirm out of the consequences!'

'I object to these proceedings. This is not justice! Your system offers no chance for the accused to defend himself, to challenge facts, to introduce new evidence. No! This is a kangaroo court run by pinko left-wing smear artists and I refuse to submit to its judgment.'

'You still don't understand, do you? We have all the facts. We know everything about you. We know the truth of your every lie, the cost of your every treachery, the object of your every lust, the source of your every nightmare, the intent of your every deceit, and the contents of every erasure on your tapes, Watergate and the rest.'

Enkidu sat back, nodded to Bryan to take over. Bryan bit into a carrot as Nixon replied.

'You're all nothing but a bunch of shit-faced cocksuckers out to get me.'

Bryan swallowed and in cold fury said, 'As president of this court I must remind you our duty is not to determine facts nor is it to determine innocence or guilt. No indeed. You have already been condemned. You have condemned yourself. Our sole responsibility here is to enquire into the circumstances so that we may determine the appropriate punishment.'

Nixon sprang to his feet and the choristers' chant swelled as he raised his hands aloft in the victory gesture of Alexander the Great.

'You don't know who I am!' Nixon bellowed. The Chorus subsided to counterpoint and he vaulted from the dock to rule the floor.

'I'm a rip-snorter and a fire-eater; I'm your man for a fight, fair or foul I'm your man! I'm a jaw-breaker and a bone-crusher! Let all the sons of men bear witness especially those cowering varmint Democrats may they size me up and shudder. I'm the maker of deserts, the wall-eyed harbinger of desolation. In school I played all-league tackle and went both ways and never took my equipment out of my locker. I won the Heisman Trophy and the Nobel Prize. On my mother's side I'm kin to rattlers and on my father's I'm kin to all the eagles and I'm full brother to the bears. I'm the blue-eyed linx of Fifth Avenue. I'm the monarch of the movies and the idol of the girls. I am a he-ICBM. My breath breeds nuclear fusion! I've crimped a cat-a-mount in Central Park with nothing but my living hands and at the Bronx Zoo I broke a living alligator across my knee! I'm the vigilante hero of the subways and I wipe my ass with muggers' scalps! I'm king of Times Square and I terrorize the dope dealers! I caught a foul-tipped comet at Yankee Stadium! I muzzled a hurricane and walked it down Park Avenue on a leash! My dinner plates were fired in Hell and I've drunk more and pissed less than any man alive! I've hugged an elephant to death and made a grizzly plead for mercy! I'm a sleep-disturber, a gum-tickler and a gale-breaker! Who'll come gouge with me, who'll come box with me, who'll come bite with me, who'll come jump me with their judo! Who dares help Bryan's court slide its knives into my back! Where's the hit man bold enough to hit me! I'm Nixon-eye the dead shot; I'm the blood-drinking skin-tearing fist-plying demon of the upper East Side! I sank four carriers at Midway! I won the Battle of Britain! I saved Shadrach, Mesach and Abednigo from the Fiery Furnace! The flash of my eye will collapse a condo and the shriek of my anger hurl trains from the tracks! I'm a slayer and a slaughterer and I cook and eat my dead! I can wade the Hudson and come out in Jersey bone dry! I can fly through the air without wings but only on hot days! I'm doom and devastation to the Democrats and the Holy Spirit rides my breath! I can imitate Irving, I'm the prince of pool and at poker two times in three I beat the Fiend himself! I'm the blossom of the Chrysler Building and I take jacuzzis with the Pope at Saint Pat's! I'm the only toot-roarer in this tee-total cosmic union who was a General and an Admiral at the same time! I have fifteen sons and they look like Swedes and they're as smart as Einstein and I'm the one who works the e-lec-tric chair at Sing Sing! I bull and bear the market as I please, may I be kicked to death by grasshoppers if that's not so! I'm rough and hardy, I'm an attack dog, a snapping turtle, a great white shark! This is *me* and no mistake! I'm Earthquake Dick who makes them tremble in Moscow and wobble in Beijing! If you fright to fight me dare to try me fair-and-square! My plea to this court is swelling in me like a drowned horse and I'm going to serve it up with thunder sauce and lightning grease!'

Bryan looked down at him.

'Have you quite finished?'

Nixon stood there, stunned.

'I don't know what got into me.'

'You may proceed with your defense,' said Bryan.

Whatever had gotten into him before, crawled into him again. He stiffened and strutted and cried out, 'I came into the world off the Staten Island Ferry riding a lion and I left it astride a nuclear rocket! At Happy Hour I drink a gallon of margaritas and then shoot out traffic lights eight blocks away! I smoke Castro's cigars and rule Broadway with a snapping cracking bull whip! I'm a wolf with a barbed-wire tail; I'm a stud with a twelve-inch spur! I win all the game shows and I'm king of the lottery and I have six Oscars and I sing at the Met! I'm richer than Chase Manhattan, brighter than the sun, more popular than Miss America, and prettier than any underwear model! My books lead the best-seller lists and I was the handsomest groom of all at this year's weddings and at this year's funerals I was the best-looking corpse! When

I get mad I snatch planes from the sky and pluck subs from the sea! When I feel playful I jump over my own shadow or blow out the moon! So you shit-faced judges you just go ahead and persecute me all you want and see how much good it does!'

He went limp again and his face expressed sensitivity, injury, surprise.

'The court will take your plea under advisement. The court also makes official note of the fact your plea no longer swells in you like the body of a drowned horse.' Bryan looked at his papers, and then back at the failed conspirator.

'Mr Nixon. The heavy heart produces astral oblivion – except in the case of shameless tricksters such as yourself. When we prepared your sentence yesterday we considered screening a movie showing you the facts of your life and their effects on others, but, upon consulting Astral Centrale, we concluded you are quite unable to recognize your own villainy, even if objectively presented to you on film. We therefore conclude if after letting you make your own plea you did not understand it was you speaking and not some imp in possession of your astral, we would zombify you, bottle your astral for display in the Halloween Museum, and dispose of your cadavre in the boiling mud pools.'

Bryan raised his gavel and struck it down.

'So ordered!'

SEVENTEEN

As they led Nixon away apprehensions of what they would do to me, about what they would judge suitable to my transgressions, mingled with memories of boiling mud pools. Not that I've actually seen any, but in my mind an image bubbles anyway. Al once visited the Boiling Mud Pools of Rotorua when the ship he was working on stopped in New Zealand, which is where Rotorua is. During a late bourbon evening at my club he told me all about them in the course of a conversation occasioned by a ghastly accident reported in that day's *Times*. The Chorus began humming 'The Death March' from Saul. The case now before the court concerned a woman who had eaten a Devil Dog in hopes of thus regaining some of her lost cadaveric density, if not animality. Over a fortnight she'd consumed it in the form of steaks, chops, roast, then stew and broth. You are what you eat. Not so, it turned out. The only result of her altered diet took the form of a summons to appear here in cadavre court. As the proceedings moved along it came to me with a sudden shock that perhaps they dispose of all contraband cadavre substance by casting it into boiling mud pools.

And that what's that would happen to me!

Yes!

At this very moment the Cadavre Disposal Officers might well be escorting the zombified Nixon across a pasture to the brink of a mud pool. My turn would come next. In this odorless place would he sense the fuming sulfur? As he trudges between the officers, his feet alone leave crushed grass behind. They lead him to the edge and tell him to keep going and with the obedience of the true zombie paying for his crimes

Nixon ambles into the steaming liquid mud and sinks out of sight.

Would they zombify *me*?

I strove against sliding down into pure panic. I could not keep my attention on the court proceedings. Al had said the mud pools have names like The Devil's Porridge Pot. They lie in a cleft between wooded hills on a plain extending before the gigantic volcano Mount Egmont, the Fuji of New Zealand, a terrestrial hernia where earth's entrails breach earth's skin and discharge massive geysers and hot springs and steam jets and sulfuric clouds and the boiling cauldrons of mud. The Maori build houses among them and use them to cook their food. The Anglos have planted grass and some trees, too, on what had been a grim and barren landscape, thus creating a union of paradise and the infernal regions. Al had set the picture as firmly in my head as any of the slides Enkidu II always made us watch on returning from his annual vacations. The accident slide flashed its image on to the back of my forehead. By the shoulder of a curve on a two-lane asphalt highway stands a low circular rim about thirty feet across and two feet high, one resembling the lip of a volcano. Within it seethes an evil, hideous mass of boiling chocolate mousse, no – burbling diarrhea, giving off noxious vapors, thin, sulfurous, upward drifting. The ground trembles underfoot. You lean on the guard rail and peer at the slowly churning muck as greasy bubbles rise and burst in puffs of steam and the only sound is an endless subtle plop-plop-plop. From an overhanging maple branch a green leaf falls and drifts down to rest on the surface and it cooks away until it is a hand of veins and is gone.

The sun fades and sets and the moon shines down its pale yellow light. On the highway headlights swiftly approach, heralding a handsome young couple in an open car drinking from a bottle, and the driver kisses his companion and misses the curve and the car speeds straight ahead off the road through the guard rail and vaults from the rim far into the pool.

And the car settles.

And as it settles screams overwhelm the plop-plopping and the young people struggle and sink.

And that is what the *Times* reported to us in far off Pacifica.

And that is what Al had built up into a slow-moving mind-painting.

And that is what we had discussed over Jack Daniels until the sun came up.

'How the hell'd that be for the start of a movie?' I asked.

'It'd put the two-by-four to the mule, for sure.' Al looked out the view window at the ocean. 'First, I'd shoot the movie with a carload of beautiful people hurtling in. Then I'd shoot it again, same moonlight, same car, only this time with old people, and then a stretch limo driven by a despicable richnik without a chauffeur, then with a chauffeur. Next time, a staff car carrying Adolf Hitler, and after that a rapist being chased by police, and then police, and cetera and cetera and I'd splice all the takes together and we'd have a whole movie.'

'Bill! We're talking to *you*.'

W. B. Antonelli glared down at me, then he smiled. Apparently I hadn't heard them call my case.

'Well, Bill, we got you while you're hot. You couldn't be hotter.'

Bryan didn't know me, and the other two had never liked me.

'Count on us to keep you hot.'

At least all three of them were good Democrats.

'Hot!'

I always find a shiny side.

'Bill, we try to be informal in these hearings.'

Where were Harding and Hale?

'Immigration,' said Bryan, 'has confirmed your identity and certified your heart.'

I'd only been one year old when Al saw Bryan the carrot-biter at the monkey trial.

'We're especially considerate of senior citizens,' said Enkidu.

I'd never in my life before thought of myself as a senior citizen.

'We'll complete the inquest in no time,' said Bryan.

Where the fuck was Al!

'You'll be out of here before you know it,' said Enkidu.

'Your worships,' said I. 'Send me back to the Other Side.'

'That may not be possible,' said Antonelli.

'W.B., it's me, your old pal, Bill!'

'That's irrelevant. We may not be formal here, but that doesn't mean we grant special privileges.'

'Send me back to my club.'

'Bill, you're asking us to favoritize you.'

'Not at all, your worship.'

'You! The guy who used to joke about hearse and re-hearse.'

'That didn't mean anything, W.B. I was only kidding.'

'You used to laugh at my urn garden! You razzed me when I'd lay out an attractive young client in my slumber room! You told folks I had a crush on the animal control officer and asked her to bring me business, dogs and cats I'd embalm in secret. Oh, you know how to make me mad, all right! You and that no good Al used to say you'd slip me knock-out drops and bury me alive. And then you got sore when Doc and me laid out Al in my best coffin! You used to leave phone calls from the dead on my answering machine! You screwed a handle on to the crown of a skull and gave it to me for Christmas to drink out of! You teased me when I supported the Right-to-Die Movement! And you kept telling me to save money by stamping DECEASED on all my bills and Bills, including me! And now, for the love of Pete, you want me to let bygones be bygones!'

The Chorus broke in:

Fingernails, toenails, appendixes too,
All kinds of things are taken from you;
Drill, razor and tweezer, scissor and knife,
Make a trail of dead parts to trace out your life.

'Your worships, I submit that justice and equity require you to send me back to my Side.'

'We are not yet at liberty to do so,' said Bryan.

'How about Al? I was invited here by Al! He sent Harding and Hale to get me.'

'Who's this Al?'

'Alvin Burke, Mr. Bryan.'

Bryan glanced at his colleagues. 'Does either of you know an Alvin Burke?'

'Yes,' said W.B. 'But I've never seen him around here, or heard tell of him even.'

Enkidu nodded agreement.

'We have an administrative problem,' said Bryan. 'Our normal procedure, after someone's been summoned here, is to verify his identity and the validity of his heart certificate, and then to compare his actual date of entry with the date preordained by the Fate Bureau. But we have not yet received your data from the bureau. Believe me, these delays are a trial to all of us. The bureau is still integrating the archives previously kept separately in Heaven and in Hell, which is difficult because some of Hell's Great Registers were stolen. As if that didn't make enough trouble, the bureau is also in the process of being computerized to interface with Astral Centrale.'

'I understand, your worship.'

'The most difficult phase of your case, the heart and identity aspect, is complete. And the hat you're wearing confirms we've classified you in the proper category: that of *Flaco*.'

'Flaco!'

'Precisely. Look at what's happening on your Side. Humanity finds itself in the greatest crisis in all of its history. It's a matter of life and death, not only for the individual but for the race. Either you and we will unite into a single family, diversity in unity – or complex life There and Here will be finished and the future belong to the insects. The next few years will settle the outcome. Our records show you have done almost nothing to influence it. Flaco! How else can we classify you? You let lunacy prevail on earth without doing anything about it.'

'Your worship. I'm just one guy. I help the Democrats. I

keep my saloon as honest and happy and healthy as I can. Surely, that's enough.'

'Perhaps, Mr. Flaco. Nevertheless, passive indifference such as yours allows change for the worst to continue. Change for the worst, sir. *Evil*-ution.'

'That's not fair, your worship. I'm a good Democrat and keep a good place and support three employees whom I treat fairly and with respect.'

'The ambiance of your El Flaco Club is not the issue. Our subject here is the death of the world.' He raised a palm to silence me. 'This court remands you to a holding cell where you will be kept in custody until we hear from the Fate Bureau and are ready to return you here for sentencing.'

He raised his gavel and struck the bench.

'So ordered! The clerk will call the next case.'

The Chorus, ironically I thought, began singing 'Brighten the Corner Where You Are,' and Henri cuffed my wrists and led me through a door at the back of the room to an elevator. Once inside, he uncuffed me and, smiling, said, 'We're going to my locker. Just walk along with me like you belong and don't say anything.' We sank down about five floors and stepped into a corridor where policemen came and went. He led me into a locker room, took a dispatch case from his locker, and brought me back to the elevator. This time, he pushed an up button. 'Mon vieux,' he said, 'in the old days we peace officers wore long capes with lead sewn into the hems of their skirts. This ingenious and useful weapon is why street people called us flics. Under the capes in our back pockets most of us carried wine to ease the day along.' Scornfully, he brushed his fingers across his tunic. 'Now I have to keep the pignard in my locker.' We stepped out of the elevator into a jail painted a tasteful designer blue-gray. Henri spoke with the desk sergeant. The sergeant opened a gate and Henri escorted me by a number of solid steel doors to a barred door which he opened. We went in and sat down together on the bottom part of the double bunk. From the ceiling outside a TV-eye peered at us. 'These cells have microphones and speakers, too, built into those overhead light fixtures.' Henri drew a liter of wine from his dispatch case. 'Don't worry, the sergeant's a pal of mine and didn't turn any of that stuff on.'

He offered me the bottle and I toasted him.

'In Africa,' said Henri, after toasting me back, 'some people believe if they scorn the divine in themselves their tools and utensils will revolt and drive them from their homes to live in the trees.' He drank again and wiped his mouth with the back of his hand. 'Me, I think that resembles what's happening with Astral Centrale. We are letting, no – making our astrals pass over into it. The cosmic central computer is becoming an astral bank, taking astral from each of us, accumulating capital so to speak. When the time is right, in one big grand giant slurrrrrrp Astral Centrale will suck all our remaining astral out of us and we'll be zombified, only worse, because we have no cadavre substance. Astral Centrale will suck our souls and we'll all die the second death and Astral Centrale will *be* humanity.'

We each took a long drink.

'So, old-timer, doesn't *that* make you shit yourself!' He grasped my arm and looked me in the eye. 'My friend, that's what *I* call evil-ution!' He drank again. 'Astral Centrale is liberating our economy from the rigid density of machinery and will soon do the same for itself. It's growing bio-factories which will in turn grow things for us like food and clothes and medicine and, yes, electronic products. Personally, I think after Astral Centrale sucks our souls, it will grow cadavre substance to embody itself. It will leave all those printed circuits and microchips and dials and screens and cabinets behind and move into flesh.' He sighed and corked his bottle. 'I wish it would grow some flesh on me.' Henri stood outside the door now, locking it. I gazed at the top bunk. 'Are they going to put someone else in with me?'

'According to the sergeant, they're going to put the Boneless Boy in here as soon as he's finished in court.'

'Tell me you're kidding.'

'You'll have to give him the lower bunk.'

Smiling, Henri walked away and left me alone.

I glanced around the cell. Nothing but the bunk, and a toilet sans seat, and the recessed light fixture which began playing soft music by the Rolling Heads, and blue-gray steel walls.

And graffiti!

An ache of homesickness surged in me.

The graffiti brought it on.

What will they do to me?

When I get back, I'll change the name of my place to the Helhevland Club.

Has a nice sound to it.

In my place one wall in each restroom is a blackboard with a piece of chalk on a chain.

The idea came from Bill Wiley's Have-You-Learned-Your-Lesson painting with the chalk hanging from it.

Each night as part of my closing down routine I erase and wash the blackboards.

I wipe away standard graffiti you've seen a thousand times: DON'T THROW YOUR BUTTS IN THE TOILET AS IT MAKES THEM SOGGY AND HARD TO LIGHT . . . SUCK MY PRICK . . . BITE MY TITS . . . LICK MINE . . . and the scatological and the bigoted and the perverse and worse. But every now and then I have to remove artifacts of the triumphant poetic imagination, some of which I'm sure splatted on to those boards straight out of Al's head.

Panic struck.

My heart thumped.

I'll never get back!

Who's erasing those boards now?

I went over to a wall.

CONNIE LINGUS LOVES PHIL ATIO

What?

HELHEVLAND SUCKS!

Ain't that the fucking truth?

Can Astral Centrale read my mind?

Detect my mind crimes?

SHIT ON MY MOMENTO MORI

What did they do with Al's squed?

BALLET DANCER/BELLY DANCER

Throw it into the mud pools?

BE MY DADA DADDY DOLL

Where the fuck is Al?

THE ONLY THING WORSE THAN A URINAL WITH LIPS IS A URINAL WITH TEETH

That's his style.

TOO MANY GOOKS SPOIL THE WAR

So's that.

His main theme, though, is theology.

Especially Satanaël: God/Satan.

Ringing in my ear is what he told me about Satanaël on one of our long after-hours whiskey nights.

'Satan and me, we're both small-<u>d</u> democrats. Our crimes are the same. Had Satan been in America at the time of the Revolution, he'd have been another Nathan Hale. A volunteer soldier, a patriot, a selfless idealist. Just like me, and you too Bill, Satan believes in liberty, equality, and fraternity, or, better, autonomy, equality, community. Because of his beliefs, and his spirited character too, he was the George Washington of God's absolute monarchy. God was one hell of a lot worse than George III. Satan had no choice. He could not go along with God's capricious tyranny. He rebelled. Of all the angels at God's table, Satan was His favorite. Satan's revolt made God so furious He flung Satan and his pals down into the depths. Then, as Saint Augustine tells us, God created man so He could raise up a few goody-goody kiss-asses who never sinned, that is never disobeyed Him, to fill the empty chairs at His table. The rest, a huge mob of sinners, He sent down to Satan. What would you think of an absolute ruler, or a father, who keeps threatening you with death if you don't obey and who keeps saying: "I show favors to whom I will; I grant mercy to whom I will."? Any man of soul and spirit would revolt against a king or father like that! Even you, Bill. That'd be enough to make even a sheep like you rebel. Yes! Believe me! God is the original Tory. He should be tarred-and-feathered! Lucifer, not God, is the model of the good democrat, the good American.'

'Then why do Satanists torture little kids and eat human flesh instead of advancing the cause of democracy?'

'Marx once said: "One thing I know is that I am not a Marxist." Freud has vigorously denied being a Freudian, and, time and again, Satan has declared, "I am not nor have I ever been a Satanist." As for you, old pal, are you a Billist?'

'Easy, easy. Lay off my case,' I said to Al. No, not to Al, to a memory.

I clambered to the upper bunk, stretched out, and closed my eyes. No noise at all, anywhere. A slamless slammer. Had some boy really made it here with all his flesh but no bones? I dozed and dreamed. Something about riding mules some-where without ever arriving. There was more to it, but that's all I can remember. Maybe because I woke abruptly on hearing the powerful but comforting voice of Radio, speaking to me through the light fixture.

'Here comes Henri to take you back. Don't trust him!'

Still giddy from sleep, I swung my feet over the edge of the bunk and sat up.

I peered into the corridor.

No sign of Henri.

I looked at my feet.

No mist beneath them, no sea of fire down there either.

Seeing it as abstract art, as an aerial view, I gazed at the spotted cement of the floor.

I slid down off the bunk and stood.

Just a good solid jailhouse floor.

'Don't try to understand. Enjoy.'

'Enjoy!'

'Don't say I didn't warn you.'

'Okay.'

'I told you not to worry.'

'What?' I asked, and, flashing *Mad Magazine*, added, 'What, me worry?'

Henri opened the door and I stepped out and he closed it with a certain insouciance, but silently.

So now we're walking along this gray-blue steel corridor.

Henri says, 'They brought you to this Side *en-cadavre* because you have no ambition and, thus, can be trusted. Why cadavre? To zombify *you*, as they told me, wouldn't take much doing. Dead while alive, monsieur. Alive while dead? Blackbeard. After they cut off his head and threw his body in the water, he swam around his ship twice. At the suggestion of Astral Centrale, old timer, they imported you to experiment with having cadavre on this Side.'

'Doesn't anybody really see me when they look at me?'

'There's something important you and I must discuss after your court appearance.'

'The Boneless Boy?'

We walked into the court room and seated ourselves in the front pew.

Justice Bryan called my case.

'We have,' he said to me, 'received the relevant data. It's in order. Do you want to make a statement?'

'I'd like to see Al.'

'We don't know any Al.'

'Boone or Fisk?'

'We don't know them either.'

Obviously they knew them. But all alone in this strange and dangerous place I was not about to contradict them.

'Nathan Hale and Warren Gamalial Harding, ex-president of the United States, are both friends of mine and I move you have them called to speak on my behalf.'

'You are trying to influence this court with matter irrelevant to your frustrated attempt to smuggle cadavre into our country.'

I opened my mouth to speak but Bryan cut me with a glare

and declared, 'This court sentences you to an indefinite term on the Looking Over Past Life Platform.' Bryan gaveled the bench. 'So ordered!'

Henri cuffed me.

'Let's go.'

The Chorus jeered from the jury box:

You've always played the air guitar.

And then came Al's voice. 'Bill, you are *hopeless*.'

EIGHTEEN

Instead of taking me to the Ministry of Punishments to complete the paperwork associated with my sentence, Henri uncuffed me and drove me to a large building modeled on a hive. We entered an extensive plaza furnished with cafés and trees and sculpture. Around it stood level upon level of stores, offices, apartments, sheltered by a transparent roof. Musak I recognized as deriving from a Dada Commando album called The Other Side set the tone. To the sound of Satanaël Boogie, Henri led me to a glassed-in elevator. Peering through its walls as we rose, I watched folks and things diminish to Lilliputian size.

When we stepped out, Henri glanced anxiously up and down the corridor.

'Can't be too careful. These halls are dangerous and nobody *ever* uses the stairs.'

We stopped before a steel door punctured with a tiny peephole and fitted with several locks, mainly obsolete, artifacts of industrial and criminal progress. Henri opened them with keys and an electronic card. We went into a vestibule. The inner door, geometric designs carved in dark wood, opened with a French-style handle. As we walked through Henri put an arm around my shoulder and said, 'Chez moi!'

Before me in his living room I saw a huge brass tray on short legs, a bookcase, a rubber plant, a TV on a chrome frame, but no chairs. Underfoot, I felt the luxury of a magnificent Islamic rug. Henri arranged some pillows around the tray and we reclined on them. He gestured at the contents of the room. 'Everything here has a special meaning. These keepsakes carry me back to better days.' Henri rose. A beatific smile shone down on me. 'I'm going to bring us something special.'

He stepped through an arched doorway into another room. On the gleaming tray stood a telephone, a cheap souvenir model of the Chrysler Building, and a framed photograph of French policemen in the old-fashioned blue uniform. A venetian blind closed over the window hid the magnificent view of Helhevland Henri must at times enjoy. A large framed woodcut displayed on the wall by the doorway showed a skeleton trio toasting each other in a medieval-Mexican *wassail macabre*. Henri, now in yellow Moorish slippers and a long blue robe, came back in and set a genuine water pipe on the shining table. Never before had I seen a hookah except in movies and the funny papers.

With reverent regard he tamped a raisin-like sacrament into the bowl.

He held a match to it and sucked smoke bubbling grayly through the water and I watched his cheeks grow pinker and his eyes turn greener and dilate. After this had been going on for a while, Henri let me suck smoke, and then ran a hand over my leg. He squeezed and then seized my shoulder and after that took my cheeks between his hands. An approach! As to an Arab boy! An old-timer like me! 'Cadavre!' he exclaimed. 'True solid flesh!' Still grasping my cheeks, he peered into my eyes. 'I want you to stand up.' We both rose. No matter where you see him, Henri comes off as a trim, strong-looking man, but draped in his Moorish djellaba he seemed downright massive.

'I want you to push my shoulder, but softly.'

I gave him a gentle shove.

He stumbled back as if he had no mass at all.

My hand encountered hardly any resistance.

'You see, my friend, we have no true substance.'

'And so you envy me.'

'I imagine the power you have over the rest of us.'

'I guess I could push you around.'

'You could push us all around.'

'I wouldn't, though.'

'No one here can kill your astral until they kill your cadavre. And that . . . well, maybe . . . with Devil dogs? For any of us here destroying you with the second death would be most difficult.'

I told him that was a relief.

'Together, monsieur, you and I, we could go a long way here. Believe me, we could. Me, I know how everything works. I know what needs to be done. As for you, you could, when necessary, apply the force.'

I sat down again on his lush carpet and he took his place across his brilliant brass table with its beaten-in Arabic script declaring There is no God but God and Mohammed is his prophet.

'Together, monsieur, you and I, we could purge Helhevland of the Exterminators.'

'That's a big order for just two men.'

'Somebody's got to do it! The Exterminators embody destruction, dissolution, ruin. They are the quintessence of sadism, rapine and murder; they are entropy manifest; they are malevolence personified. They leave a trail of rotting food, poisoned water, butchered babies, razed cities, and bloating dead astrals tumbling in the wind. Their hearts are heavy and their spirits steeped in evil. They are the soul of pain and suffering, of crime and calamity, of torture and villainy!'

'Henri, I'll have to learn more about it before I promise you anything.'

'Promise anything! Moi, je comprends, moi! What irony! The only man who has the power to destroy them is you – a flaco whose premier joy is willing submission to evil!'

'You've got me wrong. Any more of that shit and I'll walk right through you and out of here.'

'You'll never get away from me, not as long as you have what I want. I rule you. I have powers you don't know about. In Helhevland, the inanimate, this building, this table, my handcuffs, all dead matter in fact, all of it's made of self-containing energy fields. It's only the biological, the open, the stuff of life, the carnal – only the *cadavre* has no true substance.'

'So I can walk out of here and you can't stop me.'

'I can have you hunted down, and chained when you're asleep, and left in an oubliette to die in your own shit.'

'Listen, you feculent fog-blob parleyvoo, you can't scare me with that.'

'And while you're dying in your own shit, Monsieur Flaco, we'll get out the electrodes and play tunes on you. And you'll learn to love it.'

I resolved to lunge at him and secure him to the TV with his own cuffs.

'I can fix it so you can never go home.' Eyes flashing, fists clenched and gesturing, he went on telling me what he had in mind for us to do. He would run the show; I would be his instrument, a tool with life in it. As he spoke I showed my poker-face, no – my hearts-face, to cover my swelling concern about how to finesse his strong cards, avoid his Queen of Spades. He stood and began explaining how the two of us, his mind and my matter, would move against the Exterminators, and as he talked on I felt myself being battered and drenched by a cataract of lust, not for what he could accomplish by using me to effect his will, but for the joy of the using.

And then abruptly he hushed and turned toward the door.

There in the entrance to the vestibule, framed by the doorway, stood the Pathfinder, Daniel Boone.

A thin smile creased his strong old face and his dreadlocks hung like silver springs over his green-plaid lumberjacket.

'Well now, Henri, ain't this something,' he said as he strode into the room and handed Henri some papers he drew from his shoulder bag. 'Seems like you need better locks.'

Henri scanned the papers, then looked back at Boone, silent, furious.

'Come on Frenchy, it's not the end of the world.'

'This can't be.'

'Kind of like sucking gas, ain't it?' Boone turned to me. 'Those papers from the Ministry of Punishments transfer you to my custody.'

'Monsieur Boone,' said Henri, getting a grip on himself, 'can I get you a drink?'

'Sure. Whiskey. Monongahela if you have it, but any old rot gut if you don't.'

'Ice? Seltzer water?'

'No. Not for me. As they say, water's too thick to breathe and too thin to plow.' Boone accepted a glass, drank, tucked the papers back into his bag. 'Have to be getting along now.'

With Henri's angry glare piercing our backs we strode through the vestibule, by the steel door Boone had left ajar, and along the hall toward the elevators.

'Am I glad to see you!'

'Just happened to be in the neighborhood.'

'How'd you find me?'

He pressed the elevator button and we stood waiting.

'I trailed you.'

'By woodcraft through this world of concrete and machines?'

'Didn't make much use of bent twigs and crushed leaves at that.' He smiled in that gentle friendly way he had. 'When I heard you were in trouble I went to see Darrow . . . '

'*Darrow?*'

'He's a good friend of Al's and a big chief in the Ministry of Punishments.' We stepped into the elevator. 'Darrow gave me the custody papers and him and me together, we tracked you through that bloodhound computer, Astral Centrale.'

We sank down down down and people and things grew and grew and I began to think of myself as Alice in Crazyland. Out in the atrium, walking toward the entrance through an atmosphere ruled by the music of Turk Murphy's Dixieland Jazz Band, I invited Boone to stop in a café for coffee and a bite, but he said we had to hurry, and led me outside to a row of reserved parking places guarded by police. We walked past limousines and prowl cars to a black motorcycle, pin-striped in gold as was its boat-shaped sidecar. The ministry's logo on the gas tank served as a passover sign protecting it from being towed. 'My horse here's a real sweetheart,' Boone said, straddling the saddle, his springy silver dreadlocks bright in the sun. 'She's quiet as a dead crow.' As I strapped myself in he put on airplane goggles and started the motor. Catlike, the machine moved out into traffic and up a ramp onto the freeway.

'After we left you at my club, Daniel, what happened?'

'We took care of things, Fisk and me. He knows his way around in the city, and I'm at home in the woods, so together we can handle just about anything.'

The traffic was light. Even though Boone had his choice of lanes and speeds, we loafed along on the slow side. He seemed to be studying things. An old freeway, the landscaping had grown so thick and tall it seemed as if it might be the verge of a brake of infinite beauty, but I felt sure the green wall really screened an ugly slumscape. That illusion reinforced my sense of having lost all connections, all of them, save for those with the throbbing machine I sat in, the air I breathed, and the man at my side.

'Where's Al?' I asked, not at all sure if I wanted to know the answer.

'Down there where you came from, exiled maybe.' Boone took a speaker from a saddlebag, listened to it, spoke softly into it, listened again. 'I go down there every now and then, sometimes to Boonville. I like to keep track.' He ran us along an off ramp and I had a brief view of high row houses, dirty bricks, ill-repair. 'Nobody can see me when I'm down on your Side,' said Boone, 'and right now I wish they couldn't see us here on mine.' He stopped for a light and foot-traffic passed. The people, all of them, were Japanese males, young or middle-aged, clad in imperial military uniforms. 'When I'm down there in Boonville, I'm there without being there. I can't influence anything. All I can do is observe. It's like coming into Thespian Hall and walking around on stage during the play and no one notices. Makes me feel as useless as tits on a bullfrog.' We lunged ahead. 'Boonville, that's where I first saw Al.' We were now speeding between the row houses. They reminded me of Baltimore. 'I like best being alone when I can feel myself part of everything. I like cold streams and towering forests.' He flung around a corner and around another and into a garage. With a hand control he lowered the door and turned on the lights. 'I watched Al grow up. And when for adventure and honor he scorned his Boonville future and went to New Orleans and out to the eternal sea, when he did that – and I was in the school auditorium and heard his speech – when he did that, I knew we lived by the same totem, and I adopted him as my son.'

Boone swung out of the saddle and motioned me to follow him. We went up some stairs and into a kitchen. He had me sit at the table and he began to heat coffee in a tall blue-enameled pot. What Boone had said about being Al's soul-father meant I am the best friend of Boone's soul-son. I shared this thought. Boone made that flickering smile and said, 'Soul-father! Yes! I like that. Al's body-father was a smart lawyer but so dumb about everything else he thought milk comes from ants.'

He set the coffee on the table. From where I sat I had a good view of the foot traffic through gauze curtains. Boone took some cold cuts and bread from the fridge and served our snack and sat down. He looked out at the cars and the people passing close by our window. Almost all of them were sensitive-looking adolescents, boys and girls, dressed for summer.

'I hope you didn't find me rude,' he said, turning his glance toward me. 'We had to move so fast I didn't have time to explain things. But don't fret yourself. We're all right now.'

I smiled at him and began building a sandwich.

'What we're doing now is hiding from Astral Centrale.'

'Do you think that's possible?'

'Believe me, no matter what they say about Astral Centrale knowing everything, it *is* possible, and we're doing it.'

We sat silently for several minutes eating and drinking coffee. I remembered Radio's warning about eating the food of the dead, but I'd done it, and I would not worry, not in Boone's company. I asked him what this place was, and he told me all its residents had killed themselves. 'All suicides are sent here to this city of the disgraced, because they have defied the Fate Bureau's lifespan decrees. They have not completed their assigned lifetimes and that, sir, is a serious administrative crime.'

'Can they get out?'

'When they've done their time they go to the heart-weighing. Most of them don't pass. Their astrals are liquidated; the others are released into society. No reason for the bureau to be so hog-headed about that. Astrals can't kill themselves. When we get our Helhevland union greased and working smoothly, we'll get all the folks out of this barnyard and into the pasture.'

'Is this your house?'

'No, a friend's. I can come here when I like.' He finished eating and began picking his teeth. 'Nate lived in this house until I got him out of here.'

'Nate? A suicide?'

'That fellow, he had a martyr-for-liberty complex, but he wasn't a suicide. No sir. The bureau saw him as one of those marginals, a man sound as a racehorse in the flush of youth who volunteers in war for some certain-death mission. Nate was an officer, and a college boy, and a spy – the first of a long line from that spy school, Yale – and the only other fault he could have had to make him worse in my estimation is being a carrier of hog cholera – and he was a Christian, too, which ain't no recommendation either, not to me, but in spite of all that I truly like the boy. Al and me helped get him out of here. Nate was a test case. Long after he'd gone through his assigned lifespan they held him here and he'd be here still if Al and I had not spirited him out and slipped into the heart-weighing. There's one light-hearted boy for you, that Nate. I admire what he did to save the army, and the way he died, and him at Yale saying no to joining the Skull and Bones Society. To get into that aristo band you have to dig up the remains of some famous man and bring back a dry bone or two to keep in their archives. Nate is like Al. He has every gift, and he can think. If he'd lived, he'd have done a lot for the country. And I know for fair, he was getting to where he'd have no more truck with God and that sissy, Jesus, than I do.'

'I knew it! You're a pagan like me!'

'Well, sir, let me put it this way. When churches began to catch up with me, that was way back in 1800 – when that happened I went to Missouri. We had a saying then: God will never cross the Mississippi. Simon Kenton, Ethan Allen, Sam Houston, none of the pathfinders and long hunters were Christians. Not a one. And Washington, Jefferson, Madison, Franklin, Jackson, Lincoln, Franklin Roosevelt, none of them were either. It makes me cross as thunder them Christers keep schools and papers from telling the truth about who we are and where we come from! I'd rather wear a sod blanket than have to see that lie on our money!'

'Al, he gave me a sign I keep over the bar, up above the big window. IN GOD WE TRUST, ALL OTHERS PAY.' Boone smiled and fell silent and kept glancing out the window. Some of the passing adolescents wore BORN TO LOSE T-shirts. Should I tell them to be proud because it takes a loser to make a winner? Could they get a second chance, be born again, reincarnated, recycled? I was beginning to feel all the religions are right about what happens on This Side. Maybe these kids could go back and have another try. I asked and Boone said nobody knows. Maybe that's what happens to the folks whose hearts are too heavy.

Abruptly, Boone stood.

'Time to head out.'

I followed him back down to the garage. A windowless van with Helhevland commercial plates stood there and we clambered into the back and lay down on the floor.

In the driver's seat, solid, shoulders bursting his blue blazer, sat Jim Fisk.

NINETEEN

When Al was sixteen, that summer, sitting on a crate at the landing, in the vortex of labor: workers, farmers, horses, drays, trucks, riverboats, sitting there watching and hearing, out of it but in it, that's when the first clear sense of his philosophy of the moving balance of opposites had come to him. Its focus is the subjective-objective paradox. We are at once everything and nothing. Even though we feel like we're the center of all, we know, by cosmic standards, the measure of all, we are nothing. Religions, he told me, resolve this by projecting the *me* out into the *it*, and thus, with the help of metaphors, resolve the paradox by making the *me* into the *it*. But why resolve the paradox? Why not refine one's sense of being its focus, and enjoy it? Why not?

As Fisk hurtled us through the city and shadows flickered and reeled across the steel floor and turns and stops flung us about, while that went on I told Boone about Al's philosophy, and how it sustained me, especially at times like this.

The dancing shadows composed my last connection with my ambient.

'Didst thou know,' asked Boone, 'that I was reared in the Society of Friends, and am a Quaker, the same as Nixon?'

I felt the van rolling out on to the freeway.

'I've broken loose from saying thee and thou, but I still seek the sense of the meeting. Finding it – that's about as easy as using a jackknife to slice sunbeams. It comes to me, my sense of the meeting, from being alone in the forest, or from living with Indians. Lines of force form an irregular grid throughout the forest, and, I think, everywhere else. Where these lines cross their strength redoubles. Some of these crossing spots are death spots. They touch fire to powder. At those few points where the strongest lines converge and cross in profusion, you have holy power spots, and that's where you go to renew yourself, to invigorate, you'll see.'

Smiling, he lay back on the vibrating floor, and put an arm over his eyes and dropped off to sleep. I became aware of a rhythmatic throb coming from somewhere in the machinery and then of the Chorus intoning AL'S DEAD IN HIS SQUED THAT'S WHAT WE SAID AL'S DEAD IN HIS SQUED THAT'S WHAT WE SAID AL'S DEAD IN HIS SQUED THAT'S WHAT WE SAID and then the van left the freeway, and we bumped along, and I saw leaf shadows flashing on the floor, and I knew we were in the woods.

So where's the squed now?

As for Al, most of him's in the sky and the sea.

And the rest of him? In his squed deep in a mudpool alongside Nixon, cooking.

Fisk slid the door open.

We shook hands.

'How you keeping?' he asked.

'Can't complain.' He spoke with Boone, stepped back up into the van and drove away in the dirt tracks and ruts of what looked like a fire road.

'And now,' said Boone, starting off through the ferns, 'we go this way, quiet as fairy feet on beds of flowers.'

'Can you smell anything? I can't.'

'I can. I always can.'

As we moved silently through the primeval forest, this cathedral of hardwood trees, I felt swelling in myself Boone's air of easy confidence. We climbed over huge slimy logs and passed through sunny meadows and by ponds and paced through cold streams, scaring crayfish and water bugs. This was the at-home, the at-peace I remembered from being alone in Los Padres National Forest near Big Sur, alone in the company of all life, the sounds, motions, colors, fragrance – here but a memory. The terrain began rising and granite thrust through the soil and birdsong ruled. Squirrels leapt overhead; rabbits and quail started up in alarm. As we pushed our way through the tall brown grass of an open space toward a muddy pond Boone smiled and said, '*Here.*'

We sat on a polished blue boulder and looked out over the water where turtle heads were lunging up at flies and receding in patterns of rings.

'When the biochemists start growing our food in factories, we can have this back.'

He stood.

'This is a special place. Wait here. Try to hatch that stone. I have to go ahead and do some scouting.'

He quickly vanished into the woods.

Sitting there alone with all life I fell into a trancelike déjà-vu of this place. Al'd told me about it. He's out there in the field across the pond with three outlaw construction types, building a cabin. Trucks and piles of lumber stand near to them. One working stiff, Bill, always brings superb lunches assembled by his loving wife, and, jealous, the others always tease him about it and try to make him share, but he will not. Today, they arrived on the job before the dew dried off the framing. They're behind schedule and working long and fast. Bill swings some planks off a pile on to his shoulder and totters toward his comrades, and falls over, dead of a heart attack. They put him in the passenger seat of his truck, work until noon, eat his lunch, work until evening, and then go back with him rigid in his seat to report his desertion from the crew of *Spaceship Earth*.

I feel a touch on my shoulder.

Boone's there.

'Didn't hatch yet, eh?'

'No, but I kept it covered.'

'I wonder what kind of chick will come out.' He sat next to me. 'I saw signs, so I went to see. An Exterminator death team's camped up ahead. And our favorite Frenchy's with them.'

'Henri?'

'The very same.'

'What now?'

'Help's coming.'

'What do we do?'

'What we don't do is kick the ant hill.'

'That would be bad policy.'

'For me it's more than policy. I don't feel the war spirit, not ever, but I do defend me and mine.'

'Do they know we're here?'

'They've been following us, but I think we fooled them. Our government insists on being blind to it – the unthinkable thought you know – but the Exterminators' hackers have broken into Astral Centrale. Soon we'll see a war of the programs, a civil war, inside of Astral Centrale itself as our government and the Exterminators struggle to shape the tee-total of human knowledge.'

A smashing crashing sound approached in the woods.

'Don't fret yourself. That's just Charley.'

'Charley?'

'Charley's a bird, a true lady. Didn't know that till she laid an egg. Charley's a good friend and a darling.'

'How can a hunter – a *long* hunter – be a friend of *birds*?'

'These days, William, I only hunt animals that hunt meat. Charley grazes on leaves and grass. She can't fly, but she's a true cloud-scraper for all of that.'

The woods-crushing noise came closer.

'No bird is that loud.'

'Except Charley. She's a moa bird.'

'I've heard them jabber, and they're loud all right, but you can't tell me mynah birds crash through trees!'

'Not mynah, William. *Moa*.'

'Moas are extinct.'

'Not any more.'

'I know they are! Al told me all about it! They evolved in a predator-free environment, ancient New Zealand. Then man came in canoes and stayed and hunted them and wore their skins and ate them, every one, not even sparing their eggs.'

'When you see Charley, you'll know she exists. She's no ostrich in disguise. No sir! Ostriches evolved with people, so they can run a-mile-a-minute. Charley! She's pretty smart, but she's the very Eve of slow and clumsy. And her eggs! Thirteen inches long, green like duck eggs, and hold two gallons. And each one is a single cell!'

'Daniel, meaning no disrespect, but moas are extinct.'

'They were until I had a moa bone smuggled from your Side. Darrow and I sent it to Astral Centrale and Astral Centrale read the DNA code and made us some fertilized eggs, and now I have my pet dinosaur.'

'Is Charley the help you expect?'

'You might say that.'

'How about Al?'

'With luck, you'll see Al.'

Out of the woods into the meadow stalked an enormous bird. Ten feet tall at least. She ambled toward us, cropping grass, then stood in the pond, crane-like, looped neck, snatching delicacies from the water with her broad beak. She shuffled toward us on powerful scaly legs and peered at us through alert, protruding eyes. Purple-black she was with flashes of golden-buff.

She looked right at Boone and emitted a tremendous tree-shaking squawk.

Boone drew a deep breath and blasted out a squawk in reply.

Charley paced out of the water, dripping, and came straight up to Boone and lowered her head to him and he gave her a hug and a kiss.

'She must weigh more than five hundred pounds!'

'I reckon so.'

'Won't all that noise betray us?'

'Don't chafe about it. The Exterminators know moas live in these woods. Besides, William, you're like Al. You're both so lucky that if I threw you off Goat Island into the Niagara River right there at the top of the falls, you'd float upstream.'

I smiled at him, momentarily believing it.

Boone rasped articulated sounds at Charley and slapped her bare rump.

She clucked and sank into an awkward squat.

Boone pulled himself up on to her back.

He reached down for my hand and drew me up behind him.

She rose and stalked through the pond and into the woods. It was rather like riding along a rough road on top of a car, not easy but you can do it. I clung to Boone's waist and he hung on to the base of her neck.

'Are you taking me to the punishment platform?'

'Not yet.'

'Al. You're taking me to Al!'

'No.'

Charley carried us out of the woods into a vast swampy meadow alive with the astrals of every conceivable creature.

'I call this the Evolution-Devolution Zoo,' said Boone, 'though you could think of it as the Goodilution-Evilution Bog.'

'Does Charley live here?'

'I'd rather be gut-shot than see that happen.'

We were stomping over snails and lizards and toads as we advanced in the direction of towering ant hills and herds of cattle. All the astrals I could see seemed alive, but none moved or cried out.

'They're all trapped in the Shiva system.'

I noticed every now and then a creature would vanish like a popped bubble or appear out of nowhere.

'This is a replacement depot. They're all waiting to be reincarnated over on your Side. The astrals here are getting used to their new shapes, the bodies they'll move into down There when their new body is born.'

Sacred cattle and dogs roamed through the absolute hush and stillness of this strange arklike precinct. That the air was pure produced in me an infinite gratitude for the odorless nature of Helhevland.

'They get reborn up and down the food chain, depending on whether they've been good or bad in their last life.'

My anxiety redoubled.

Why had they brought *me* here?

'A truly heroic devotion to self-purification can carry these astrals to the top of the food chain and beyond to be born as humans – untouchables, servants to the higher castes.'

Charley lurched and I saved myself by grasping Boone's springy dreadlocks.

Annoyed, he glanced back at me, then smiled and said, 'As they range up and down the food chain and the caste ladder, these astrals are striving, hoping, to get out of their bodies altogether and turn into air!'

Charley began to trot across a patch of porcupines.

'Folks here in this astral swamp, they all *yearn* for the second death. They dream of it; they work for it. This place is the blood daddy of the big suck Astral Centrale is going to pull off some day.' He looked back at me. 'When Astral Centrale don't need servants any more, and when he's sucked in all human knowledge, why, then friend, then he'll suck in all the astrals too, and that will finish off the human race. People will have built their own Exterminator. Astral Centrale, himself, will be the next branch of human evolution. That's why I call him Brahma-Nirvana the Second. These astrals here are seeking oblivion, soulicide, the second death. *Trying* for it. As with most things on both Sides, what these folks believe looks better on the menu than it does on the plate.'

As he spoke and we swayed along I was becoming more and more aware of a soughing wind-sound.

'It don't even look good on the menu, this astral soup. When they arrive at human form these food-chain rangers live to purify themselves: Yoga, breathe water, draw water up your asshole and squirt it out your ears! Why? To clean yourself out! Range the food chain, purge your guts, sing everything in the key of *me*. All so you can turn into air and be extinguished!' Pulling back on Charley's neck, he made her stop. 'Friend, I'd rather be snake-bit than pant after that!'

Abruptly, the wind-sound was beating overhead and I looked up and saw a helicopter. Boone comforted Charley with soft squawks and affectionate strokes. The pilot blew a hunting fanfare out his window on a gleaming cornet, then set the chopper down close beside us. We slid down from Charley's back and went over to this other bird. The pilot sprang out, warm and smiling.

Warren Harding!

I embraced him, then shook his hand.

'Where's Nate?' I asked.

'Back at the ministry.'

I stood there, hands on his shoulders, smiling. 'First a president – and now a pilot!'

'I'm tickled to death to see you.'

'And a helicopter pilot at that!'

'Well now, Bill. Flying whirleybirds ain't all that hard, really. Not for me. I'm one of those fellows can do most anything. You bet! You should see me play first base!'

Boone drew my custody papers from his back pocket and returned them to Warren.

'Aren't you coming?'

'Reckon I'll stay here with Charley.'

'In that case,' said Harding, taking a golden fountain pen from the pocket of his golf jacket, 'you'll have to sign off.' Boone signed, then said something to Charley, and Charley subsided into a camel-like squat. Boone clambered up on to her back. Soon, remembering the glass elevator, I was looking down from the rising helicopter, watching as Charley and her rider diminished to Lilliputian dimensions and vanished in the astral zoo below.

Boiling mud pools of Rotorua

PART FIVE

AL'S

STOOL

Stools are traditional seats and symbols. In some places a man's personal stool is regarded as the shrine of his soul, and in funeral ceremonies it is carried to the family stool house, where regular offerings are made to the spirit of the ancestor.

Geoffrey Parrinder, *African Mythology*, London 1967

TWENTY

All the while we were rising up out of the woods, Harding chattered at me and sucked a cigar, puffing the smoke at a fly. Suddenly outside the window, more gray. We'd joined the fly in the clouds. 'Yah-*haaaaaaaaaa*, here we go!' Warren flung the copter forward into the opaque nowhere, our destination: my punishment. 'Daniel's friend down there, now that's what I call a *bird*. Birdwise, that babe can't be beat!' Warren lifted his cornet from the floor and polished it on his sleeve. 'Wanted to meet you at the depot with a brass band, all wearing El Flaco hats, but this was the best I could do.' He blew a violent fanfare. 'I see you still have your hat, Bill. That's the spirit. You bet it is! Don't cave in. Boost your business through thick and thin. Nothing succeeds in business like success.' As he babbled on and we flew over invisible possible futures, I reflected on the similarities between Warren and myself. He's emotional and imaginative. He hates being alone. Warren, and Nate, too, trusts to the decency in people. Like Boone, he dislikes violence and loves animals. He respects labor, its rights and dignity. But all this is one person at a time. He never sees the big picture, just the details. And he believed — still? I wonder — the people who own the country ought to run it. He put the horn to his lips and played 'Sugar Blues' as we zipped over the cloud-shrouded potential futures below. He's a mamma's boy. He's loyal to friends. He's a gambler and a speculator, much more so than me. The wailing shock of cornet music inside the metal chopper vexed me. Warren's no more a Christian than I am. But excepting Jimmy Carter and, maybe, John Adams, what president was? Harding concluded his solo and smiled at me. 'That should raise the dead.' He spit on the floor. 'A riddle. Why is Helhevland like orchids and mushrooms? Why? It thrives on death. Don't knock it. Death works for us, you bet! So, Bill, grab a good thing when you see it. Sing your Death Song, and stay.' He blew a fierce high-note leading into a medley of bugle calls. Somewhere far below our possible futures moved by, unseen. He paused to drain the spit out of his horn.

'Warren,' I said, 'the cornet's the most arrogant instrument in the whole fucking world!'

'Not compared to the bazoon.'

'Bazoon? What the hell's that?'

'It's the Devil's instrument.' He glanced at me. 'To the bazoonist it sounds like the music of the spheres, but to the ladies and gents within range it's fingernails scraping blackboards, it's squeaking hinges and boiler factories. Coming out here to this Side when we stopped to eat we should have stayed longer and heard Beelzebob's Bayou Bazoon Band. He's got them all, the tenor baz, the alto baz, the string baz, the bass baz, and the real killer, the bull baz. He's got a singer, too.' He slapped my back. 'Tell you what. You fly this baby for a while.'

Warren shed his jacket, dropped it on the deck behind him, and began sliding out of his seat. Appalled by all the controls and instruments, I gripped him by the suspenders and held him in place.

'No way you'll get *me* to fly this windmill.'

He laughed and relaxed.

'Guess you'll just have to trust yourself to a regular Republican, then.'

'Some day Warren, you'll learn. Everyone — even you — is a Democrat. A good Democrat. Only some of them don't know it yet.'

'So when you going to sing your Death Song and join us?'

'Never.'

'Look back there.'

I turned.

In the back of the chopper, sitting assembled on the deck, the Chorus!

'Son-of-a-bitch!'
'Sing out, fellows! Carol it for old Bill!'

Life is but a dreary picture,
Sad and dismal as the tomb,
Life is but internal stricture,
Life is but a fallen womb:
Uncle Ted is constipated,
Aunty Flo is doing time,
Brother Fred has been indicted,
For some gross, perverted crime.
Oh, life is but a dreary picture,
Devoid of laughs, devoid of smiles,
As here I sit in discomfiture,
Cracking ice for grandpaw's piles.

'That's the truth, Bill. Your Side is all balled up. It's a mess. So are you ready to join us as a regular citizen of the United Republic of Helhevland?'

'Be serious.'

'The only thing I really miss from your Side is running my newspaper. That's what I really like to do. I enjoy all phases of the newspaper business, and I'm good at it, too. Makes me feel at home. Here, I can play golf, and baseball, and music, and bloviate with just about everybody you ever heard of, but they don't have newspapers here. They don't really have *news* here, either. This place is, well . . . different.'

'You folks haven't got it together yet.'

'No. For us, it's Articles of Confederation time. We are developing our constitution, yes, and we've formed our union, and believe me that wasn't easy, but we still have a long way to go. I think of us as pioneers and founders.'

'And what happens here depends on what we do on my Side.'

'That's it.'

'So our hope is your hope.'

'Yes.'

'There's a lot of good people on our Side.'

'There's a lot of love and honor here.'

'Down home, too.'

'Bill, for a Democrat, you've got a pretty good slant on things.' He was slowing our forward motion to a hover. Out of the haze before us abruptly loomed a pole and a flag: the trilobite banner of the Republic of Helhevland.

'I get a kick out of the good old flag. Makes me feel all warm inside.' Our whirling blades had blown the mist and the flag into turmoil. 'I take to this place like a duck to water. And that even though – and you know it's a funny thing, even though here in our cosmic union, in our republic, we don't have Republicans. The bright side of that is we don't have Democrats either.'

We sank slowly in the mist and perched on a helipad built on to the top of a building. Attendants in blue coveralls took charge of our steed. I followed Harding to an elevator cupola and soon we were sinking down inside the building. We stepped out into what I judged to be the basement. Slouching as usual, Harding led the way to a high security area and gained admission with an electronic card. Presently, we came to a door with a red light over it; the whole impressed me as being very like the entrance to a television studio. Harding opened the door and I found myself on a balcony overlooking a huge, bottomless, circular lens. A platform reached out over it on a hydraulic arm at whose base stood a console of controls. And there! Rising from his seat behind the console, brushing crumbs off his mouth: Nathan Hale!

He'd been eating dumplings.

He gave me a warm smile and a firm handshake.

'We lost track of you for a while,' he said in his sharp, piercing voice.

'How long did you wait?'

'Hours. Then we called Darrow and picked up your trail.'

'What happens now?'

'We have to execute your sentence. You have to go out on the Looking Over Past Life Platform.'

He had me lie down on the platform, my head braced over a secondary lens, a telephone set taped to my cheek and ear. 'They brought you here as an experiment. The idea was to see if a heart enveloped in *cadavre* substance can pass the weighing test. And everything would have worked out smoothly if you hadn't brought that squed along.' He was hunching down beside me. 'It's going to be all right. Don't fret about it. Darrow selected the program cards himself.' Nate explained how the cards would slide into the program slot in the console and focus the lens. 'I'll tell you the names of them before I slide them in.'

He rose and walked back to sit at the console. Harding stood beside him. With a low vibrating hummmmmm the arm extended and carried me out over the exact center of the enormous lens. What I could see resembled what's visible from an airplane just over the clouds. In my ear, Hale's voice, 'You'll soon be watching earth and its follies, much like my old friend, Lucian.'

'Lucian?'

'Eighteen hundred years ago he visited the gods on Mount Olympus long after earth people'd stopped believing in them. From the summit, they all peered down at your Side. What Lucian wrote about that experience earned him the number one spot on the Catholic Church's *Index* of forbidden books. Him and me, we love to play with this instrument of punishment.'

'Yeah, all right, Nate, but let's get the show on the road.'

'We have a monitor here, so we'll see everything you see.' He paused. 'Looking back on your past life, taking the long view, we go behind you jumping off your forebears' shoulders, to your first ancestor – the first living cell. So here we go with your first card, the one called Long View.'

I lay there for an endless time enthralled by this exhumation of my roots. Tailor-made for me by Astral Centrale, it took the form of a movie, one more dramatic than documentary, because Astral Centrale knows drama is more to my taste.

My only self-conscious moment came as a spasm-urge to piss, but it soon subsided as music and dialog and Nate's commentary and the sounds of nature surged through my fancy along with the moving pictures. And how did they look? How to explain them to you? I'm peering down into that bottomless lens and what I see there, the images, are in three dimensions, shimmering. I'm looking at them through heat rising behind an antique window. No. I'm gazing into the depths of a tropical sea through the transparent bottom of a boat. But it's not that, either. Holograms! Yes! Holograms. I'm spellbound by holograms moving in the deep.

Nate shows me the first cell of life evolving just as I had evolved in my mother's womb from egg to infant. I see the first cell of life growing into domineering reptiles, and I see catastrophe sweep them away. I see dinosaurs rise to mastery, and then, save for birds, I see cataclysm destroy them all. I see mammals rise to take their place and man advance in the footsteps of his invented gods toward dominion over all life.

I see a million people worldwide, living in small tribes, in balance with nature. Swelling in them soon to burst forth is the idea man can alter nature to make it more hospitable to his survival. He tames plants and animals and remakes their environments so they may thrive and he may thrive upon them. 'Now,' says Nate, 'watch as tribes, all of them republics, confederate and unite and grow two independent civilizations, those of China and of Egypt/West Asia, where, through science applied to work, power over nature waxes, until humankind unites into a single world order, *Res Publica Orbus Terrarum*, or is killed by nature and insects inherit the earth.'

I saw the peerless cruelty of feudal warlords ruling over their peasant tribes, and of emperors rising from warlord leagues, and I saw these emperors, armed with machines, ravage the tribes of the world.

And I saw in America, in France, in Russia, in China, great revolutions against warlord rule.

And I saw the great revolutions slide from the hands of

artists into those of megalomaniacs and administrators who resonate with the warlord order.

This, history, his story, her story – my story, *my*stery, from before there was a *me*, moved me immensely. A young Druid draws the burned piece of the bannock and is sacrificed to the gods who thusly chose him, and his carcass is thrown into a bog. Now it's images from both American continents, utterly pristine, twenty thousand years ago, before the first human beings came. I see USS *Enterprise* running aground in Oakland and heating to the edge of meltdown because its cooling pumps are sucking mud. A detachment of British soldiers lost in a South Carolina swamp during the Revolution still wanders there two centuries later seeking the way out. George Washington rides his huge white horse back and forth between battling armies and no one ever shoots him. Year after year on the Western Front, in the trenches, amid decaying bones and rotting flesh, millions of men fight to the death with rifle, bomb, knife, and bayonet. Men with a trenching machine dig a grave and cover the raw dirt with artificial grass and watch the last rites from behind the bushes as they wait to fill the hole and steal the flowers. A stench permeating the top floor of a Chicago parking structure draws an attendant who, glancing into the back seat of a Ford, sees a dead woman covered with newspapers. Jungle life in the slums of old London and the shanty towns of Mexico City – Devil's Island – the Australian prison colonies – the war galleys in Barcelona – slave auctions in New Orleans – coal mining in crawl-tunnels under the Irish Sea – rebels twisting on gibbets in the Irish air – adolescents following dreams of stardom to the Los Angeles Greyhound station – rain- and cloud-forests falling before bulldozers along the equator – torture experts being trained in my country at my expense – flaming German tanks caught refueling by Soviets emerging from the sewers of Stalingrad – a death march in Cambodia – card after card passes through the console creating an avalanche of images tumbling me down down down into anguish and despair and when I feel I must surely break, the lens clears and Nate's voice sounds in my head.

'Against that, William, I set the amazing increase of the world's population since the Revolution. Mark it! That upward curve accelerating all the time represents man's increasing success against his enemies.'

Another program card slipped into place. 'This one is called Boonville. Astral Centrale must think you are partly a product of your mentor, Al, although I cannot truly say. Maybe it's Darrow's idea. Some of this is as new to me as it is to you. I can't read Astral Centrale's mind. I don't know why the platform is programmed for you in the way it is. I do know, though, that Astral Centrale does not influence my comments.'

Images appear and move again. I see Al's forebears in the Revolution riding with Light-Horse Harry Lee's cavalry and filing through the woods with Morgan's riflemen. Burkes come out to Missouri, to Little Dixie, and they farm with slaves, but free them when the war breaks out, and go to fight for the Confederacy. I see Al as a baby and then a child and then an adolescent, looking much like Billy, or for that matter, Nate. He's with a girl on a porch swing; he's walking through blue-grass pasture bright with daisies to the woods to pick wild strawberries; he's eating apple pie with cheese; he's swinging between crabapple trees on a barrel-stave hammock; he's by a flaming hot woodstove helping his mother make plum preserves for the winter; he's riding in a child-sized wagon pulled by a goat; he's on the roof oiling the gilded-rooster weather vane; as he walks among the six thousand residents of Boonville under the shade trees or ambles through the halls of school by the lockers he has a smile and a kind word for everyone; he's playing cribbage with his father; he's driving his father's Pierce-Arrow to a school dance; he peers into a drugstore window at people drinking their morning whiskey; he leads a girl called Sally through spring air along Morgan Street past his house to the site of the Second Battle of Boonville where, after a vicious fight, Confederates overran a force of Chicago Germans and Irish, and he loses his virginity behind some bushes; he passes by the two-storey columns of Thespian Hall at Main and Vine where the Lyric theater is showing the latest Chaplin movie; he whoops with mirth reading Mencken in his father's copy of *American Mercury*; he strolls by Kemper Military School and thinks in awe of its alumnus, Will Rogers, whose column he reads every day. The more I wander with Al by brick houses and gingerbread Victorians and down the cobblestone decline of Main Street to the corncob pipe factory and the tall brick and frame warehouses and the boats at the landing, the more I see of Al, toddler, child, and man, at work, on errands, at school, at home, at study, at play, the plainer it becomes Al could have grown up to hold dominion, in Boonville, in Jefferson City, even in Washington.

And now, did any of it matter? Now that – as he would put it – he was as dead as a ship in port.

'Yes. And the ship resurrects when the engines start.'

More Al cards passed through the console. Al walked off the *California* with Joe Curran to begin the thirty-six strike, and sailors in all the ports hit the bricks, and walked picket lines, and fought fierce battles with goons, until finally the National Maritime Union was established. In ports around the world Al was the darling of the sporting girls, especially at his favorite destinations, Spain, France, Italy and Greece – the Romance Run. And from time to time gales and ice-storms and typhoons and hurricanes and, eventually, warplanes and warships, interposed themselves between him and his favorite sweethearts, the distaff part of the sailor's family, the sporting girls, called whores by people who don't know any better. As all this swirled through my head I realized more than ever Al's story is one of adventure and survival, a young man's story, yes, one whose theme is the finessing of arrogant authorities.

'Now comes a card with your name on it.'

My flaco story.

Some of it I'm proud of, and some is embarrassing, too fucking embarrassing! I'd forgotten it until these images were recalled. Above all, my story is dull. It contains but one event of my making, my breaking loose from Chicago and coming to California. Compared to Al's story, mine is nowhere. Al is a son of the Confederacy and a son of the Revolution whose bloodlines go deep into colonial Virginia and Maryland. I can only trace my family back to grandparents who came from somewhere in the Austro-Hungarian Empire. My story is nowhere and no-where. Well, at least it's typical of the no-where stories which form the vast majority of the biographies of my fellow Americans. Skokie High. Chess Club. Stamp collecting. Track Team. Thoroughly undistinguished service during the war, mainly in Illinois. Then, clerking in liquor stores, and now, saloon keeping. I writhe with embarrassment as my program card makes me watch me watching TV almost every night. I see my barren wife Margaret, who left me and moved to Los Angeles. When I phoned her about six months ago a record told me her number had been disconnected. Last week a letter returned to sender – me – marked Address Unknown.

My unlived life.

But isn't a lived life a luxury?

One enjoyed at the expense of others?

Were we all practising romantics, who'd do the work?

And now deep down in the lens I see the sailors and me leaving Death alone and naked by that dark Nebraska roadside. Death sits in the adjacent cornfield until dawn, then lopes through it toward the farm house, and snatching an axe from the woodpile rushes through a flutter of chickens up the back steps into the kitchen and the farmer looks up from his breakfast just in time to eat the axe blade.

And then in a welter of blood, Death pushes the farm wife back against the stove and with immense strength forces her face down on to a flaming burner.

Tiring of her gasping shrieks, Death grasps the breadknife and cuts her throat.

He helps himself to scrambled eggs, bacon, muffins, and after pouring a glass of milk, he sits at the table and eats. Then he goes upstairs, showers, dresses in the farmer's best suit, takes all the money and the truck keys, and drives off eastward between dew-bright cornfields toward the glory of the rising sun.

And now, abruptly, before I can react, I'm looking at images of Pacifica, all the familiar stores and streets and buildings, and at the freeway cleaving the town in two and, everywhere, I see people I know, and life goes on as usual, but without me, as if I'd never existed.

Does anybody miss me?

And now the scene shifts to the interior of the El Flaco Club.

I'm looking at a party.

The guests are dressed in Renaissance style.

It's a Dead Al Party!

With a Renaissance theme.

That's what it says on the posters.

'Nate! You're showing me the future!'

'No. That's only 1992. Don't you remember? On this Side we're in the twenty-first century; we're inaugurating the Third Millennium.'

'Good news we've made it that far.'

'That's no news. We're only one of the possibilities.'

Down at the party nobody seems to miss me any more than they do out on the streets. Billy just leapt up on the bar and called for silence. He introduces Doc and Two-Twelve Heather, his co-directors of the A.L. Foundation, and welcomes everyone.

'Who's that fellow looks like me?' asks Nate. 'That man wearing the big, floppy beret?'

'That's Billy.'

'Of course! Al told me all about him. I've always wondered what Al's son looks like. Me! Me in my party mode.'

'Al's great-grandson.'

'No. Son. When Billy was born, Al was over sixty; the great-grandson part is just the cover story.'

It took me a while to digest that.

The first time I saw Billy he was a toddler riding in the bottom part of Al's market cart along with a bag of potatoes and he was humming the sacred Celtic chant of the Lady of the Underworld, the one we know as 'Sing a Song of Six-pence.' Billy was now sitting on the bar, smiling at Heather, who stood before him. He pushed his beret way back on his head. 'A working-class romantic,' he said. 'That's me.'

'You're not working class.'

'An every-class romantic, that's me.'

'You're not a romantic.'

'Whatever you say.'

He swung himself over behind the bar, dashed along the duckboards to the other end, took down Al's lute, came back and around to sit at the corner, by where Heather stood next to my empty stool. He played Heather a sweet Beatle song. He's good on the lute. He never did learn how to play the saw, though, so it will hang there behind the bar, rusting, mute, until someone throws it out. Al learned how to play it from Tom Scribner, an old-time logger whose statue you can see in Santa Cruz, and he brought the secret with him when he followed Tom to this Side.

Billy raised a highball glass to Heather.

She raised hers to him.

'As Al used to say to you, Billy, anything you can imagine, and more, can come true in your lifetime.'

'A libation to Al,' he said, pouring his drink on to the floor.

'A libation,' replied Heather, pouring hers.

By now I'm really feeling left out. Sorry for myself. Melancholy. Nobody misses me. Life goes on as usual. Without me. I've been utterly and totally superfluous. Nobody remembers me. I've had no effect on the world. Except my folly killed those two farmers. A profound shudder and sorrow aches through me. Me, already I'm nowhere. Al! His bequest conferred immortality. They pour libations to Al's astral, but not to mine.

How can there be a worse punishment than seeing the truth?

'And now,' said Billy, refilling his glass and raising it, 'a libation to old Bill, the man I was named for.'

AL'S STOOL

He dumped the drink. I looked him in the eye and filled his glass from my bottle.

I raised my glass in wassail: 'To you, Billy, a gentleman of the Third Millennium.'

'To the captain of the El Flaco Club.'

TWENTY-ONE

The beret had fallen off Billy's head and he wore ordinary clothes, his DEADHEAD sweatshirt and jeans. Festoons of orange, and black, and white bunting hung from his neck, down his back, and his shoulder bag rested on the bar-rail at his feet. 'I want to decorate Al's stool with five-ball colors to celebrate the start of its new career.' We were alone. 'And I'll brighten up the rest of your bar-room, too.' Black night reigned outside my view window; the lute reposed in its place on the wall. 'I meant to surprise you. I was going to drop in through the skylight. Break in, even. But you left the door open.'

'Did Al really name you for me?'

'That's what he says.'

I nodded, smiling, pleased, and trying to forget the open door.

'Because I have your name, sometimes I feel like you. A captain, in control, you know, confident, on top of it, the customers and running this place. But most of the time I feel like Billy Budd.'

'As of six a.m. you're captain of the A.L. Foundation.'

'You won't be disappointed.'

I smiled my agreement. Billy crouched and wrapped the pylon of the stool with bunting, talking as he worked.

'Al said stools are a big deal in Africa, below the Sahara where the black people are. A man's stool is his throne, his shrine, and now that we've adopted the custom right here in Pacifica-by-the-Sea, let's change the name of your place to Al's Family Stool House, and let regulars keep their personal stools — the round part, I mean, on shelves under the bar.

And when they come in they can swap the house stool for theirs and we'll hustle more endowments, and you'll be world famous, and stoolism will become a universal fad, a cosmic craze.'

Billy spun the stool, stood to look at it, made adjustments, then, satisfied, perched on it.

'After you left me at China Basin to come back here, I helped furl *Ruby*'s sails, and then went to some bars, and drove back home. I couldn't sleep, so I opened a bottle of Al's best cognac, and drank, and tossed our antique baseball, and played his blues records, and remembered Al until it seemed as if he were there telling me things. Like he reminded me I descend from slave owners. *Slave owners*. Me!'

'I descend from Central European misfits of some kind.'

'I had this feeling Al was really there and me, well, I was in a place like stamp-album pages, like library shelves, where the living mix with the dead. He kept saying, There's got to be more than just this, and I kept saying, There is! There is!'

'Don't bet on it.'

'He kept telling me because I'm gifted and lucky and healthy and applying myself, and because I'm a son of the American Revolution, it's up to me to make the American dream the American reality. If you don't, he asked me, who *will*? And I told him I don't know if *I* will, but I'll sure as hell *try*.'

'What did he say about me?'

'He calls you his watchpartner and says making America come true is up to you too, and that you try, but it's mainly up to me.'

'The Revolution has been double-crossed so often it's turning into its opposite.'

'And even so, it's still happening, and it's still itself.'

'We've left its direction to foreigners who don't understand it. But we don't understand it any more, either. Sometimes I think we don't even care.'

'Al said our newspapers keep getting better and that racism is dying and that all the arts are flourishing, and that's partly due to the sixties survivors growing up and taking over.'

'Well, maybe. At least we don't have hicks any more.'

'The American dream. For the whole world. Al says that's what the Revolution was about and still is about. And the dream? What is it? The dream says everybody deserves a living, a dignified living – everybody. And everybody should be able to cultivate their gifts, you know, education and all that – and everybody should be free to express themselves. Yes. To have the dignified living, the cultivation, the expression, to have all that, you have to have jobs for everybody, and self-government as in every man his own king, and civil rights to guard the borders of every man's kingdom, and check-and-balance through law restraining the outside authorities, so you get justice, which is both equity before the law and a rough equality of power, political and economic, no rich no poor, no masters no slaves.'

'If the nukes don't get us, the war germs will.'

'So what?'

'So why bother?'

'So why the fuck not! Al says our job is to finesse World War III long enough to remove its causes. And that means long enough to make the American dream prevail.'

'Billy, the whole fucking thing overwhelms me. I ain't on top of it, no way. Things are changing so fast . . . Me, I'm from a different time. You? At least, you're raised to it. You *are* it.'

'And you're an old fart!' He stood, smiling, and gripped my shoulder. 'You're a fart-faced old Flaco boss.'

'And you're a fresh-faced sentimental punk!'

He carries his bag to the pool table, takes out some bunting, and begins winding it around the legs. Through the view window I see dawnlight slowly illuminating the sandy stage. The day's play will soon begin. I rattle the ice in my glass. My painting with the chalk hanging from it still advises me to learn my lesson. My anchor tattoo still shows pale blue on my wrist. Lucky Al's dead and gone, left me here to sing his song. Evolution marches on, but too slowly to notice. Boonville probably really exists out there someplace. I saw it mentioned in the *Times*. They spelled it right, too. A man from Boonville walked away from an airplane crash through deep snow and brought help to the survivors. Yes. Al has gone back down the Dani Creation Hole and I'm still here, about to ruin myself by starting out on one of the most insane adventures imaginable. I see Al smile with a flash of gold tooth. That gold must have coated all his cremains – gilded kitty litter. Shit! Dead, he's taking over. At six a.m. the El Flaco Club will metamorphose into Al's Family Stool House and my peaceful life will be forever shattered. I'll be in trouble all the time. Billy will be back in college, at U.C. Berkeley, with a great story for his friends. I'll be here every fucking day with Al's ghost rubbing my face in the shit. Free drinks on that stool! Dead Al parties! Just imagining it appals me. Jim Fisk warned me. The whole thing fermented Billy's imagination too. But Billy hadn't been flaco enough to let the dream trippers kidnap him to the Other Side. So Al had come to him. Maybe tossing an heirloom baseball's the way to make things happen. Me, I'll have to stay up all day and tonight as well to handle the inauguration of Dead Al's perpetual wake.

Lucky Al, that is.

How lucky can you be after you've found your death spot?

My best friend has bequeathed me a perpetual headache.

I'll close early. When I get too tired, I'll run everybody the fuck out!

And then that imaginary fucking Chorus will come back and yell SHAME at me.

It's bright and sunny out on the beach now. Heather will soon be here to open the bar-room for business. Billy's passed out at a table, head-on-arms in a nest of orange bunting.

And out on the beach the play begins.

The first actor is somebody I hate.

Enkidu II is out there walking his senile Devil dogs, Ego and Id.

He often comes out real early to walk them so they can shit all over the beach and he won't get caught.

The E & W Club opens at eleven.

I get all the early business.

The Other Side!

Boone and Hale and Harding and Fisk.

Talk about your whiskey nightmares!

Somebody hugging me from behind.

I smell perfume.

'Heather!'

'Jesus Christ Bill, you look like you just went through a dry carwash.'

'I've been in the boiling mud pools.'

'What?'

'Almost time to open.'

'You're telling *me*?'

'I don't exactly have it together right now.'

She kissed my cheek and went off to hang her coat and get things ready.

Enkidu paused to let one of the dogs squeeze a long loaf out on to the beach.

Heather came back with a Bloody Mary for me and some cheese crackers on a plate for us both.

'So what's with Sleeping Billy and all them Halloween colors you put around here? You trying to kill Billy so you have another candidate for sheriff?'

'Something like that.'

'Something like what?'

'Something like Al's will says the day after we dispose of his cremains we have to start the stool. Something like five minutes from now, Al's cremains take over my life. Whoever sits on that stool, we've got to give them complimentary drinks and eats. Not *free*, mind you. Complimentary. Free drinks are illegal, but these get paid for every month. By the Al Foundation. Fight it in court and we'll be fighting everybody who entertains clients with a Martini lunch, uses credit cards for drinks, or signs for drinks in bars and hotels and private clubs.'

'Who'll be the first guest of the Al foundation?'

'Ask me tomorrow, and I'll tell you.'

'This is going to be *fun*.'

'Fun!'

'Fun to see how you handle the mess you've been sucked into. You think boiling mud pools are bad! Wait till you see what comes out of this!'

'You like the dim view.'

She laughed in my face, but she's an old pal, and likes to tease, so I didn't care.

'Why,' she asked, 'do you suppose Al didn't endow a stool when he was alive?'

'Tell me Heather,' said I, although answers, all of them distressing, were running through my head. 'Why?'

'Because he didn't want to wreck his favorite bar before he croaked.'

Maybe so.

'It's a sick joke played by the dead.'

'No, it's not. Al was a good friend, a friend you could trust.'

'Al's from Missouri, the Show-Me State, right?'

'That's true.'

'And you're from Illinois. Right?'

'Right.'

'The Sucker State.'

I ground my teeth at her, then laughed. 'You win. It's six o'clock. Turn on the signs and open the door.'

She did so and came back.

'Here we go!' I said. She poured herself some coffee out of the Silex and raised her cup. 'We're in the game now!'

She began washing and polishing glasses. This was Thor's Day morning. I like to call the days by their proper names. On Thor's Days business is often slow. We might have to wait a while for the first customer. Heather came back with more cheese crackers. I began telling her about my trip to the Other Side, about Harding and Hale and Boone and Fisk, and the flying Buick, and the heart-weighing, and Henri, and the Exterminators, and the food-chain zoo, and the United Republic of Helhevland ending Satan's Secession movement by restoring his Confederacy of Hell to the Union and removing all the old leaders, including Jehovah. whom they keep in a cage on the Capitol's steps to serve as an example to the young. The more I told her, the crazier it seemed. But, determined to get the rest of it off my chest, I told her about the judges, and the boiling mud pools, and my punishment on the Looking Over Past Life Platform, even the part about the murdered farmers, and how we should have tied up Death and taken him to the police or even killed him.

She received all this making faces and shaking her head.

'Bill, you're out of your mind.' She pointed at Billy. 'That boy went to your travel agent and signed up for the same tour you did. Look at him! He's on it now, at this moment, flying around in a Buick, or eating at Beelzebob's.'

Heather's always been good at bringing me back to reality.

'Would you look there,' she said.

I turned and saw Enkidu II striding in from the street.

He must have taken his dogs home and come back.

He walked right up to Al's stool and sat on it and twirled a couple of times.

'I'll have the house specialty, one of them zombie astrals. And seeing as it's free, use your best Dutch gin, you know, the de Kuyper's premium.'

'John, how the fuck'd you hear about Al's stool?'

'Al didn't exactly keep his plan a secret.'

Heather served him a brimming drink with two straws.

He sucked, and spit on the floor.

'That's rum!'

'I thought you asked for a zombie cadavre. I must have misunderstood.'

I tried to make small talk with him, but I can't stand the sight of him. I always see him seated on that dead girl's rump, planning her disposal.

'Bill,' he said in that disgusting voice of his, between slurps on his zombie, 'You're going to be seeing a lot more of me, maybe every morning. You know how it is. I like good booze, but I don't like to pay for it.'

He winked at me and ordered another.

I could start pushing good booze on my stool clients – the very best. I could make big bucks that way. For shame! That's what Enkidu would do, were he me.

Enkidu swung off the stool.

'See you folks tomorrow morning.'

He signed for his drinks, then strode out like he owned the place.

'Heather, bring me the phone.'

'Going to call your sweetie?'

'I'm going to call the Laborers' Union and tell them to send a man over to tear out all the fucking stools.'

'Chicken!'

'That stool's going to precipitate World War III!'

'They'll have to rip out your stool, too.'

'Bring me the fucking phone.'

She took me by the hand, linking us, her fat arm flat on the bar, and peered into my eyes.

'If you can't stand the heat, you can always have the stools ripped out. All bullshit aside, the truth is, Al endowed that stool because he thought it would make enough action to wake you up.'

'So okay, I'll keep them. They're vets of World War II, 1940, classic art deco.'

'Art deco? With all them evil rivets? Flashy gaudy art deco! When I look at Al's stool, I see the Devil's birthday cake. Don't you get it? As long as that stool's doing its stuff, you'll never be bored. Thanks to Al, you'll live till you're dead.'

Heather released my hand and went back to washing glasses. I'd been feeling right along something was missing, something was wrong. Out on the beach two women played catch with a soccer ball. I looked at all the particulars of the familiar scene, the painting with its hanging chalk, the pool rules, the lute, the musical saw, the radio, the TV, my binoculars, Al's squed . . .

AL'S SQUED.

Al's squed is gone! Gone! Where the fuck is it? I'd set it on the sill last night when I came in, and nobody's been here since except Billy and Heather. I describe it to her and ask if she's seen it and she says no. I shake Billy awake and ask him and he says he hasn't seen it since I left *Ruby* and got into my car. I go behind the bar and look everywhere. The top of the squed is missing from the trash! My bowling bag is gone too, and so are most of the Flaco hats! I run outside to the parking lot.

My Buick is gone! Vanished!

I look up and down the street. No Buick.

I run to the corner and look up Park Street.

Hardly any cars at all yet. None is blue like my Buick.

I walk back inside the club.

There, at the bar, conversing with Heather, stands a man who looks like Billy from behind.

But this man has long silver dreadlocks.

APPENDIX

Translations from the Nathan Hale story:

Dulce et decorum est pro patria mori.
    How sweet and noble it is to die for one's country.
Fluctuat nec mergitur.
    It wallows but does not sink.
Neque hinc nec nunc.
    Neither from here nor from now.
Violati fulmina regis!
    The lightning of the king's violated power.
Hilaritati ac genio dicata.
    Consecrated to hilarity and to genius.
    (This is a conventional Roman army drinking toast.)

ACKNOWLEDGMENTS

Photographs of *Ruby*   Side view, Carlo Viti, rear view, Richard
Spindler. These prints of *Ruby* are
courtesy of Joshua K. Pryor, captain
and owner.

Skeletons   Michael Kane Miller. Sculpture from the
exhibition 'The Day of the Dead,
Tradition and Change in Contemporary
Mexico', shown at the Monterey Museum
of Art, California, 1985.

Nathan Hale   Michael Kane Miller. Bronze statue, City
Hall Park, New York, NY. The image on
the ½-cent postage stamp, first issued in
1922, is taken from identical Hale
statues at Yale and in Hartford,
Connecticut.

Warren G. Harding   Full-faced image is from the regular
1½-cent stamp first issued in 1930. The
profile image of Harding appears on the
2-cent memorial issue of 1923 and on
the 1½-cent regular stamp of 1925. The
other two Harding appearances on stamps
are the $2.00 Harding of 1938 and the
22-cent stamp of 1986.

Heart Weighing   This image is from 'The Egyptian Book
of the Dead' as reproduced in *The
Encyclopedia Americana*, IV (New
York, 1932).

Lute Player   Frans Hals's 'Merry Lute Player' is oil
on canvas, 35½ by 29½ inches. It was
painted circa 1627 and is in the Oscar
B. Contas collection.

Boiling Mud Pool   The long view is from the
Globus-Gateway Australia & New

Zealand travel brochure for 1986/7. The closeup is from the National Publicity Studios, 125 Lambton Quay, Wellington, New Zealand.

Al's Stool   Pen-and-ink drawing by S. Clay Wilson.

Daniel Boone   This stamp, the only one devoted to Daniel Boone, came out in 1968.

Flying Buick   Pen-and-ink drawing by Spain.

Black Flag   Designed and flown by Bartholomew 'Black Bart' Roberts, a pirate, circa 1700.

ABOUT THE AUTHOR

Richard Miller describes himself as an independent social philosopher who writes. Jobs he has had include merchant seaman, foreign correspondent, grave digger, peace campaigner and college professor. In his mid-sixties, Richard Miller lives in California; he has written two previous novels, *Amerloque* and *Snail*, and a history, *Bohemia, the Protoculture Then & Now*.